Mail Order Mismatch

Book Fifty-two in the Brides of Beckham

Kirsten Osbourne

Chapter One

Joy Miller ran through her father's wheat field as she hurried home from a long day of work, picking strawberries for a nearby farmer. She hadn't been able to get a job taking care of children as most of her older sisters had. No, she had one of the worst reputations of any of the demon horde, as the community called her and most of her siblings.

She loved being outside. She loved gardening. She was filled with unspeakable joy as she rushed home, thinking that it was time for her to find a husband. It was a daunting process because of her reputation, but she had a secret weapon at her disposal. As one of the youngest of the Miller children, she knew she could do what many of her siblings had done. She could go see her sister and be sent out as a mail-order bride.

Oh, to be the wife of a farmer who could spend her days in the fields helping him with the pure joy that came from growing things. Abruptly, she changed directions, paying no mind to the fact that she was barefoot, and her legs were covered in dirt. She wasn't going to marry anyone from Beckham anyway. No, she'd marry a farmer, she hoped.

She ran all the way into town, not stopping before she'd reached her sister's house on Rock Creek Road. There she knocked on the door, her eyes lit up with excitement at the very idea of marrying a stranger. Most women would find such a prospect daunting, but not Joy. No, she loved the idea of being a bride.

When her brother-in-law, Bernard, came to the door, she grinned up at him. "I want to see Elizabeth about becoming a mail-order bride!"

Bernard couldn't hide his smile. "Joy, your enthusiasm is a breath of fresh air around here. Most women come in and feel like it's their last hope. But you—only you—feel like you can change the world with your smile. You will make a wonderful wife for a good man."

"Well, then tell Elizabeth she'd better send me to a good one!" Joy said with a laugh.

"She's in her office," Bernard replied, opening the door wide. "I'll get tea and cookies."

"I want milk with my cookies!" Joy told him. "Who drinks tea with cookies?" She ran past him and opened the door to her sister's office without bothering to knock. "Elizabeth!"

Elizabeth looked up from her work with a smile. "Joy. What brings you here!"

Joy walked to the sofa in her sister's office and plopped down, crossing her legs and showing off all the dirt that covered her feet and calves. "I've decided to take the plunge. I need a husband."

Elizabeth laughed. "I think you need a bath more than you need a husband."

Joy wrinkled her nose. "I spent the day harvesting strawberries at the Hunt farm. I love strawberries."

Elizabeth nodded. "I can see that. You've stained your chin with some of the berries that probably should have ended up in a basket and not your mouth."

Joy giggled. "They were so good!"

Sighing, Elizabeth looked at the letters on her desk. "I don't have any farmers who are looking for a wife at the moment. A couple of ranchers if you're interested in being a rancher's wife. There's a banker in Boston who needs a wife, which would have you close enough to visit more often..."

"A banker? I wonder if he has a garden I can dig in!"

Shaking her head, Elizabeth dug through the letters until she found the one from the banker. "Maybe? Here's his letter. Read it and tell me what you think." Elizabeth was unsure if sending her tomboy sister to marry a banker was the best idea, but perhaps it would work out. Joy was so true to her name that Elizabeth was certain she could bring happiness to anyone. "How on earth are you ever going to fit into Boston high society?"

Joy grinned at her sister. "Who says I have to fit in? Maybe Boston's the one that needs a bit of shaking up!"

Elizabeth chuckled. She handed her sister the letter that had come from the banker in Boston and watched the play of emotions on her face as she read it.

Joy's eyes scanned the letter, her brow furrowing as she absorbed the words. "Well, well, well," she muttered under her breath. Leaning back against the sofa, she couldn't help but laugh. "It sounds like this Thomas could use a bit of *joy* in his life, doesn't it?"

Dearest Mrs. Elizabeth Tandy,

I am, as you may know, a man of finance. My days are filled with ledgers and numbers, my nights with the echo of ticking clocks and rustling papers. Yet amidst the arithmetic and solitude, there is a longing—a longing for companionship, for warmth, for shared smiles and shared life.

In seeking a wife, I yearn not just for a partner, but for a confidante and a friend. A woman who possesses not just beauty, but a depth of character. A woman who carries within her the strength of kindness and the courage of compassion.

In my position, I am often called upon to entertain clients of a certain social standing. It is here that I seek a woman who can navigate these waters with grace and charm. She should possess the poise to entertain, the wit to engage, and the wisdom to know when to simply listen. Her laughter should fill rooms.

She need not hail from the upper echelons of society herself, but she must be comfortable amongst them.

I believe, Mrs. Tandy, in your ability to find this woman, a woman who can stand by my side in both the quiet moments and the crowded rooms. A woman who can share in my joys, soothe my worries, and create a home that is not just a place of residence, but a sanctuary of love and warmth.

Thank you for your assistance in this deeply personal matter. I await your response with bated breath, hopeful for the future that your expertise may help me build.

Yours faithfully,

Thomas Worthington

Joy wrinkled her nose as she looked down at her bare feet and the mud caked on them. "He'd probably expect his wife to wear shoes, wouldn't he?"

Elizabeth shook her head. "I don't know what to even think of that question, Joy. Of course, you need shoes! And now my floors need swept and mopped after you left your dirt all over them."

Joy sighed. "I'll run home and tell Ma I'm marrying a fancy banker in Boston. She won't know what to think!"

"You need to write him back. You can't just show up and tell him you're his bride. Well, I guess you could, but it would be better if a letter went first."

Joy accepted the pencil and paper her sister offered and wrote a letter of response. She tried to sound less...well, less like Joy when she wrote it. She was certain the man wouldn't be happy with a girl who had mud caked on her feet and legs. No, she needed to be more Elizabeth-like. But that made her smile. If Elizabeth could look like a member of the upper class, then so could she!

Dear Mr. Thomas Worthington,

After reading your letter, I can't help but feel a connection forming.

Your words, so eloquently penned, resonate with a sincerity that warms me more than the afternoon sun. You speak of a longing for companionship, and I find echoes of my own dreams in your heartfelt sentiments.

I am a simple girl, Mr. Worthington. I find joy in the simple things in life. The rustle of leaves, the crow of the rooster at dawn, and picking ripe fruits. Yet despite my love for these simple pleasures, I am not a stranger to the complexities of life. I understand the importance of your work and the role I would be expected to play.

While I may not be versed in the etiquette of high society, I have always believed that kindness, sincerity, and a genuine interest in others are the truly important part of any social gathering. I am confident in my ability to adapt, to learn, and most importantly, to bring a touch of warmth and joy to even the most austere of settings.

Your desire for a partner who can stand by your side in both quiet solitude and crowded rooms resonates deeply with me. I believe that every moment, whether filled with laughter and conversation or steeped in silence, holds its own unique beauty. I yearn for a companion who values these moments as much as I do.

The prospect of becoming your wife, your friend, your confidante fills me with a sense of hope and anticipation. I am eager to step into this new role, to learn and grow with you, and to build a home that is a sanctuary of love, warmth, and shared dreams.

Thank you, Mr. Worthington, for considering me as a potential partner in this journey. Your letter has brought joy to my day, and I look forward to the possibility of bringing joy to your life.

Yours sincerely,

Joy Miller

Joy read over her letter once before handing it back to Elizabeth, who immediately sealed it. "This will go out with tomorrow's post, and hopefully we'll have an answer soon," Elizabeth told her. "But in the meantime, I think you need to move in with me, and we'll make you some clothes that will be better suited to being a banker's wife. I have a sewing machine, and we'll get things done much faster here than we would at home."

Bernard interrupted then with cookies. "Cookies, tea, and milk," he said as he carried them into the room.

"I have to run home and tell Ma I'm marrying a banker in Boston!" Joy said. She took one of the cookies and drank the glass of milk down with one gulp. "Thanks for the milk and cookies. You're my favorite brother of all!"

Elizabeth and Bernard were left staring after Joy as she ran from the house. "A banker's wife?" Bernard asked. "Our Joy?"

Elizabeth nodded. "Who needs a dose of Joy in their life more than a banker would?" she asked.

*****

Just a few days later, Thomas Worthington sat at his desk, going over the day's agenda when a letter arrived. Frowning at his secretary, he took it and opened it with curiosity. As he read Joy's response, a small chuckle escaped his lips. "Well, she certainly has a way with words," he mused to himself.

He quickly penned a reply, trying to strike a balance between formality and warmth. Thomas knew he had to make an effort to connect with Joy, even through letters. After all, she was to be his wife now, and despite their unconventional start, he was determined to make it work.

As he sealed the envelope with his response, Thomas couldn't help but wonder what kind of person this Joy truly was. He knew there was more beneath the surface. With a newfound sense of optimism, Thomas sent off the letter, requesting that Joy come to him the following weekend. That would give him ten days to prepare a small wedding ceremony.

He could already picture the beautiful woman who would step off the train and see him standing there waiting for her. Would she find him attractive? He hoped she would because he needed Joy in his life. And now that he'd received a letter from his potential bride, he knew that joy must always be spelled with a capital J. For she was the one who would bring him the joy he craved.

*****

Joy and Elizabeth were working on her third "banker's wife" dress when Bernard came into the room with a tray of milk, cookies, and tea. "There's a letter for you, Joy," he said, holding out the paper with a smile.

Joy stuffed an entire cookie into her mouth before taking a swig of her milk. She took the letter and read over it quickly. "He wants me there next weekend. He's planning a small wedding ceremony for a week from Saturday, and he'll meet me at the train station."

Elizabeth smiled. "I think we can have three more dresses done by then. You'll have five to start out with. You'll need to find a modiste there as soon as you arrive for more dresses, though."

Joy's eyes widened. "I'm a simple girl. I don't need more than five dresses!"

Elizabeth shook her head. "Oh, but you do! You'll need five Sunday dresses alone."

Joy shook her head in disbelief. "But I've never owned more than three dresses at once."

"And from this day forward, you will need many more than that," Elizabeth said simply. "And that cookie you just ate whole is the last one you will ever shove in your mouth that way. I know it's all right to eat that way on the farm, but you'll be living in Boston, and the expectations will be very different."

Joy sighed. "I guess we're making more dresses then. At least I get to pick my own fabric!"

"And you'll want to be careful with the fabric you choose as well. No red. Red would surely single you out as a wanton woman. You're going to want subdued colors as a banker's wife."

"I guess..."

Bernard grinned at Joy. "Listen to Elizabeth. She does know what she's talking about Joy."

"I guess." Joy took another cookie, carefully taking small bites. "Better?" she asked.

"Yes, now if only you'll wait until you've chewed your food before speaking..."

"But..."

"No buts. I know we were raised differently, but I'm going to do my best to teach you some manners before you get on that train to Boston." Elizabeth's gaze made it clear she wasn't joking at all.

Joy spent the next week learning all she could about acting like a proper lady. The night before she left, she went out into Elizabeth's back garden and sat quietly, praying that she was making the right choice. She knew her life would have to be led in a more stifled way, with how she presented herself to others being of the utmost importance.

One last time, she removed her shoes and walked through the plants, carefully pulling weeds. Elizabeth had a gardener, and the man did a wonderful job, so it was hard to find any weeds, but Joy managed. Soon, she'd be embarking on not just her first journey on a train, but she would be changing her entire life. Hopefully for the better, but whether it was better or not, it would be a huge change.

As much as she was ready to marry and have children, she wasn't sure if she was ready to be tied down to a man who was a banker. Was she making a mistake? She hoped with everything inside her that she wasn't.

Chapter Two

Joy clutched the window frame of the rattling train. She peered through the smudged glass, mesmerized by the blur of unfamiliar landscapes that whisked past, a tapestry of greens and browns giving way to the encroaching cityscape.

"Bet you've never seen anything move this fast on your farm, huh?" quipped a portly gentleman across the aisle, his mustache twitching with amusement.

"Only when the pigs realize it's bath time," Joy shot back. She'd always had a knack for finding humor when she was nervous.

As the train pulled into Boston, her grip on the window eased. She smoothed out the wrinkles on Elizabeth's dress. It wasn't Elizabeth's wedding dress, but a formal white dress her sister had worn for some event in town. She'd given it to her to keep, and Joy knew she looked her absolute best.

When she stepped off the train, she immediately began looking around her for Thomas, and she wished she had a photograph of him, so she would be able to spot him among the throng of people.

Boston was a large bustling city, a big contrast to the small town feel of Beckham. There were horse-drawn carriages as well as several automobiles. She'd never been in an auto, and she imagined for a moment what it would be like if Thomas drove one. She could even hear the distant call of ships from the harbor. She was excited to see the ocean for the first time. Even though they hadn't lived very far from the ocean, her parents had never thought it was necessary to drive and see things like that.

"Wow, those buildings are tall," Joy muttered, craning her neck.

"Looking for something in particular, miss?" asked a street vendor. "Or just admiring our fair city?"

"Bit of both, I think," Joy replied. "I'm here to marry, so I'm just taking it all in."

"Best wishes to you!" he replied to her.

"Let's see if this farm girl can bloom in Beantown."

Thomas Worthington's nerves felt as if they'd get the best of him. He clutched a bouquet of carefully chosen flowers he'd gotten from a local florist. He said a silent prayer for calm and for his bride to like the flowers he'd chosen.

Around him swirled the usual flurry of the station—travelers bustling, porters shouting, steam hissing from the pistons of an idling train—but Thomas might as well have been alone for all he noticed. His gaze was fixed on the platform where the train carrying Joy would soon arrive.

When the train finally screeched to a halt and the passengers began to disembark, Thomas held his breath, searching for the face that matched the tintype photograph he'd studied so intently. And then, there she was—Joy Miller.

"Mr. Worthington?" she asked. Her eyes were the first thing he noticed. They seemed to be filled with joy. Her name did seem apt.

"Miss Miller," Thomas replied, extending the bouquet. "Welcome to Boston."

"Thank you so much," Joy said, accepting the flowers with a grin. "They're beautiful." She buried her face in the flowers with obvious enjoyment.

"The church is just this way," he said, offering her his arm.

Within moments, they were in front of a congregation of witnesses. "Friends," the minister began, addressing the small gathering in the modest chapel, "we are here to join this man and this woman in holy matrimony..."

Joy stood beside Thomas, fidgeting slightly under the weight of the lace and silk that felt foreign against her skin.

As they exchanged vows, Joy's hands were steady, while Thomas's trembled ever so slightly. When prompted to present the ring, Thomas fumbled with the tiny velvet box, eliciting a giggle from Joy that spread through the room like ripples on a pond.

"Sorry, the ring appears to be a tad nervous," Thomas apologized.

"Silly ring," Joy teased gently.

"I think I've got it," he said, finally sliding the ring onto her finger.

"I like the sound of that," Joy admitted, her smile bright enough to light the chapel.

"Then by the power vested in me, I now pronounce you husband and wife," the minister declared.

"May I kiss the bride?" Thomas asked.

"Isn't that why we're all here?" Joy quipped, tilting her chin up.

He kept the kiss brief, barely brushing his lips against hers. She caught the back of his neck and pulled him back when he went to pull away. Finally, she smiled up at him. "I think I may like you, Thomas."

He led her out to an automobile as well-wishers threw rice at them. She giggled as they left the church, perfectly content with the man beside her. He seemed a little shy, but that was nothing she couldn't handle.

On the short drive to his home, she held tightly to the seat, afraid the thing would throw her to the ground. They couldn't speak as it was too loud, and she quickly realized she preferred a horse and carriage. He stopped the automobile in front of a large home with a perfectly manicured lawn.

"This is it!" he said. She gratefully took his hand to get down from the auto, thinking she hoped she never had to be in one again. They were impractical and very uncomfortable to her way of thinking. When they reached the door, he carried her over the threshold.

Inside, he immediately introduced her to his housekeeper, Mrs. Graves, and then to two of the maids. Joy had no idea how many servants he had, but she had a feeling there would be nothing left for her to do all day. What did a woman do when they had no work?

He gave her a tour of the large home, and she was surprised to see five bedrooms. Why, there was even an indoor water closet, something she'd only seen in her sister's home.

"This house will take forever to clean!" she said, thinking about the work of simply mopping it. Her sister Elizabeth's home was the largest she'd ever been in, but this one dwarfed it.

He laughed, shaking his head. "That's why there are so many servants working for me." He paused for a moment. "For us."

"I don't know if I'll be able to get used to having servants. What does a woman do if she's not cooking, cleaning, and gardening all day?"

He chuckled. "I'm sure you'll be able to figure it out quickly."

Joy wasn't so certain. "It's a beautiful home," she said softly, feeling more than a little overwhelmed.

"I'm glad you like it. I had the cook prepare a special meal for our supper tonight, hoping to make the occasion just a bit more memorable for you. I do hope you'll like it!"

"I'm certain I will."

He led her to the dining room and pulled out a chair at the foot of the table for her before walking to the head of the table to sit. She frowned. "Why are you sitting so far from me? How will we talk?"

He frowned. "This is how people sit when they eat."

She stood up, picking up her plate and piling the silverware on it before moving to the other end of the table to sit perpendicular to him. "There. Now we can get to know one another while we eat."

"You can't move when we have people over."

"Of course not," she said. "This is simply for when we have a meal with just the two of us."

He thought about it for a moment before nodding. "All right. I think that's fine."

Their meal came in then and the maid serving it smiled when she saw that Joy had moved. She said nothing, but there was definite approval in her eyes.

Joy took her first bite and smiled, nodding. "I'm not sure what it is, but it's delicious," she said. She'd never been fussy about food, and the meat wrapped in some sort of pastry didn't phase her even a little.

"It's beef wellington," he said. "My favorite dish."

"I'll keep in mind that it's a favorite," she said, thinking forward to the time when she'd have an opportunity to cook for him.

As they ate they talked about everything and nothing at all. She was thrilled with how easygoing he seemed to be and how natural it was to talk to him.

After the meal, they retired to a parlor, and he sat on the sofa, patting the seat beside him. She sat down happily and looked at him, wondering why they were wasting their time in the parlor on their wedding night. Shouldn't they be ripping one another's clothes off? She'd never been married, but many of her friends were, and the way they talked, the wedding night was for one purpose only.

"The meal was delicious," she said, trying to think of something to say to break the ice. It was as if he became a whole new person when they moved into a new room.

"I'm glad you enjoyed it. How was your trip here?"

"Long," she said, smiling. "I'd never been on a train, and I was sure the rattling was going to keep my backside tingling forever."

His eyes widened at her mention of her backside, but he didn't reprimand her for it. Surely, she knew that she couldn't talk that way around his co-workers or clients. "Did you sit with someone kind?"

"I sat alone, but I really enjoyed watching the landscape pass by my window. In a way it felt like I was sitting still and all these things were flying past me. Of course, I know that's not what happened, but it's how it felt."

While they sat there, she kicked her shoes off and sighed happily. "My feet will never learn to like shoes."

"But...surely you've always worn shoes."

She shrugged. "Only when I have to. I wore them to church, of course, but I went to a small country school, and they were just a suggestion there, so I rarely wore them. I just can't seem to like them like other women do. My sister Elizabeth has eight pairs of shoes. Have you ever heard of anything so wasteful?"

He blinked. "I hope you know to wear your shoes in public here. The streets can be filthy at times."

"Yes, of course, I'll wear my shoes." At least she would always wear them while he was looking. It wasn't something she would do without prompting.

"So what would you like to do this evening?" he asked. "I have books, and we could read, or we could play chess...or..."

She laughed softly. "It's our wedding night. There's no need to find something to do. We're supposed to do each other. Well, that was rather crude. I just mean, we should be exploring one another..."

He chuckled. "I wasn't sure if you'd feel comfortable making love so soon..."

"I enjoyed our kiss, and you're my husband. It's not something I've ever done before, but it's meant for us to do that together."

"I suppose you're right," he said.

She reached forward to pick up her shoes. "I'll let you lead the way to the bedroom then."

Thomas didn't have to be asked twice. He was more than happy to take her to the bedroom and start their wedding night. He stood and held a hand down for her to help her to her feet, and she happily took it.

When they reached the bedroom, he opened the door wide. "This was always my father's room, and my mother's room was next door. You may have her room if you'd like."

Joy laughed. "Now why would I want to sleep alone when there's a tall, handsome man in the next room? No, I'll be sharing your room with you."

He felt the corners of his mouth curl up with a smile. "You're something pretty special, aren't you, Joy?"

"I don't know about that, but I don't think we need to be worrying about making love together. We're married after all." She dropped her shoes onto the floor and reached up to remove his suit coat. He was a little surprised, but he stood still and let her get it off.

It didn't take him long to get into the spirit of things, even though he was visibly nervous. Slowly, they undressed each other, fingertips brushing against fabric with a delicacy neither knew they possessed. The layers of Joy's gown fell away, leaving her standing bare in the moonlight that crept through the window. She watched as Thomas's formal attire was discarded piece by piece, revealing the man underneath the banker.

"Never thought I'd get you out of that suit," Joy teased.

"Only for you," Thomas replied, pulling her gently toward the bed.

As they lay down, their nervousness was palpable, a tangible entity between them. Yet, as their bodies entwined—their lips meeting in a kiss that was tentative at first, then growing more confident—they found a natural rhythm.

Afterward, as they lay together, a serene stillness settled over the room. Joy listened to the distant hum of Boston outside their window—a symphony of carriages and late-night revelers—and felt a world away from the quiet of the countryside she'd left behind.

"Everything all right?" Thomas asked, sensing the shift in her energy as she lay pensive beside him.

"Just thinking," Joy murmured, her head resting on his chest. "Big city, big buildings...big changes."

"Change can be good," Thomas offered, stroking her hair.

"It'll be good if I can figure this big city out. I'm a country girl at heart."

His chuckle vibrated beneath her cheek. "My money's on you, Mrs. Worthington."

Lying there, with the steady beat of Thomas's heart under her ear, Joy felt a spark of excitement for what was to come—a life filled with love and laughter, and perhaps a touch of the unexpected.

Thomas rolled over in bed, drawing the cotton sheet up over his shoulder as he watched Joy's silhouette against the dim light of dawn. She stood by the window, one hand resting on the glass, her posture a mixture of contemplation and resolve.

"Can't sleep?" he ventured, his voice still husky with remnants of sleep.

"Too many thoughts," she replied without turning, her gaze fixed on the awakening city.

"Care to share?" Thomas asked, hoping she'd rejoin him in bed.

"Nothing much." Joy finally turned, offering him a smile that didn't quite reach her eyes. "Just wondering how we're going to blend my country girl ways with your big city ways, I guess."

Thomas patted the empty space beside him on the bed. "Come here, let's talk about it."

She obliged, crawling back into the warm cocoon of their bed, tucking her head under his chin. "I worry we're just too different to make things work," Joy told him as she snuggled up against him.

"Perhaps," Thomas started, "but I don't think we need to borrow trouble. You'll get used to living in the city, and I'm sure we'll be happy."

"Promise me something, Thomas," Joy said, her tone serious despite the lightness of their exchange.

"Anything."

"Promise me we'll always find a way to laugh, even when things get tough."

"I will always do my best," he said.

Chapter Three

Thomas sat in his office later that day, trying to balance a column of numbers. His mind wasn't on his work. He thought back over the last twenty-four hours and the woman who had become his wife. His Joy. She was right that they were from very different backgrounds, but he knew he wanted her at his side. She could learn to be the kind of wife he needed.

"Thomas?" came Joy's voice from the doorway.

"Ah, my dear, I was just contemplating our... unique situation," he confessed, gesturing for her to join him.

"Unique's one word for it," she laughed, perching on the arm of his chair. "So, what's the verdict? Am I too much of a wildflower for your manicured gardens?"

He glanced down and noticed her bare foot dangling in the air. "Never," he assured her, his hand finding hers. "I was merely thinking about how I might bridge the gap between your world and mine."

"You mean you'll take off your shoes as well?" she asked, grinning at him.

He groaned. "I was just thinking you should put your shoes on!"

She laughed. "But...I like being barefoot. I was just looking out over the back garden. You need a swing out there, so we can sit and enjoy nature."

He shook his head. "Are you ever going to let me work?"

"Sure. You have certain hours you can work every day, and I get you the rest of the time." She leaned down and kissed him quickly. "Come outside with me."

He laughed. "I suppose since it's our honeymoon weekend I can do that. I really will be working a lot of hours though. I always have."

"So, you're going to work a lot, and there are many servants to do all the wifely chores. So, I will..." She left her sentence trailing, hoping he would fill in the blanks for her.

"You'll find hobbies," Thomas suggested.

"I know. I'll plant a kitchen garden. Then we'll save money by not having to buy everything from the market," Joy said, loving the idea.

"We don't need to save the money."

"But it will give me something to do..."

"There's an orphanage in town. You can volunteer."

"They'd let me garden, wouldn't they?"

"I'm certain they'd encourage it. It will save them money."

"Then let's go for a walk and you can show me where it is. I'd love to help them out as long as they let me dig in their dirt." And not wear shoes, she added to herself, but he wouldn't have to know about that part of things.

"Go put some shoes on, and we'll go for a walk then." He shook his head. "We've been invited to supper at a colleague's house tomorrow evening. He and his wife want to get to know you."

"Oh, I'd like that. I like the idea of making friends."

Thomas thought about her words while she hurried to get her shoes and put them on. He wasn't sure what his colleague's wife would think of Joy, but he hoped it went well for her. And he hoped she could manage to keep her shoes on. It didn't seem to be her way though.

She returned wearing the same shoes she'd worn the day before. They were obviously broken in well. "We should buy you a new pair of shoes," he said.

"Why?" Joy looked down at her feet. "There's plenty of wear left in these, and if I get new ones, I have to break them in all over again."

"But you could gift those to the orphanage."

"I'm sure the orphans don't want to wear shoes any more than I do," she said, grinning at him. "Come on. Let's walk!"

As they walked through the streets, she noticed the smell coming from some of the smokestacks in town. "Boston stinks a little," she whispered, not wanting anyone else to hear.

He laughed. "Between the industry and being right on the ocean, it does at times."

"Someday, I'm going to take you to Beckham where I grew up. The air is fresh smelling..."

"It doesn't smell like cow manure?" he asked, because that's the scent he always equated with the countryside.

"Well, sometimes, but at least it's a natural smell. Not like the smell of industry." She held onto his arm and did her best to take short steps so she wouldn't outpace him, but what she really wanted to do was run. Perhaps he wouldn't mind if she ran in their garden. Or in a park. People ran in parks even in the city, didn't they?

"I'm not sure I agree that the smell of manure is better than the smell of industry, but you can believe that if you want."

She shook her head. "There's manure on the streets of Boston. What's the difference?"

"Our manure is cleaned up."

He made no sense to her, so she changed the subject. "How far away is the orphanage?"

"About a five-minute walk from here. About fifteen minutes from home."

"That's not bad. I can walk that every day with no problem."

"Well, you probably shouldn't commit to every day. Maybe two or three days per week."

She sighed. "And what will I do the other two or three days while you work?"

"You can read books. Sew. Embroider. What did you do before you moved here and married me?"

"I had a job picking strawberries for a while. I just helped with planting or harvesting. Whatever was needed at the time."

He frowned. He hated the idea of her doing physical work like that. Didn't she know ladies were delicate? "I didn't realize."

She nodded. "My parents are farmers. Pa grows wheat. We have a couple of cows as well. Some pigs. Chickens. I was raised in the country, planting and harvesting. I enjoy working with plants."

"I'm sure they will be thrilled to have your skills at the orphanage."

"I sure hope so," she said. Joy wasn't sure why he had a problem with an honest day's work, when he was a working man himself. It just made no sense to her.

He stopped walking and pointed to a large building with a sign in front saying, "Foundling Home."

"Can we go to the door? I want to see if they need help."

He nodded reluctantly. "We can do that." Already he was seeing that his new wife, while she brought him much joy, was going to cause him some trouble. She was determined to be busy all the time. The women he knew were content to spend their time reading novels.

They walked to the door, and Joy knocked enthusiastically. An older woman, with a spreading middle, came to the door and peered out. "Oh, good. I was worried you were dropping off a child."

Joy shook her head. "No, I'd like to know if you need help."

The woman looked Joy up and down. "You look too fancy to work here."

Joy laughed. "Trust me, I'm not. I'd love to help you garden or really do whatever you need. My husband and I married yesterday, you see, and he thinks I should sit around doing nothing all day while he works."

"I'm Mona Graves. And you are?"

"I'm Joy Miller...er...Joy Worthington. I'm going to get used to my new name. Soon!"

Mrs. Graves laughed. "Well, we'd be happy to have you, Mrs. Worthington. Our volunteer who usually works with the garden is off having a baby, and she doesn't plan to come back. We'd be happy to have your help."

Joy clapped. "Oh, that's wonderful! Is it already planted? Or do I get to do that?"

"It's planted. Come, and I'll show you."

Thomas stood for a moment, feeling like the women were already fast friends. He could do nothing but tag along behind them. When they reached the garden, Joy talked about everything that needed to be done. "I need to weed all the vegetables. Oh, I love to weed. Will there be children who can help me, or will I be on my own?"

Mrs. Graves smiled. "Well, we can do it either way. Have you worked with children before?"

"I'm the fourteenth of sixteen children. I guess my only real experience with children is being one myself."

"Then I'll leave it up to you. I can send out the older boys who are harder workers or you can teach the younger children."

"Either way. If the older boys have jobs in town, I'll make do with the little ones."

"My oldest children are thirteen. As soon as they turn fourteen, we find them a job. The boys go work in factories, and the girls usually go to textile mills."

Joy frowned. "That's sad. They should be allowed to be children longer."

Mrs. Graves nodded. "I feel the same way, but there's no room for little ones if we keep the older ones."

"I see," Joy said, but she still felt sad for the children. "I'll be back in the morning, and we'll get some of the garden taken care of. I can work every day until it's caught up."

Thomas cleared his throat. "I would prefer you only commit to three days per week at most."

"Then I'll promise to be here three days per week, and I'll do my best to come the other two days as well. Will that work?"

Mrs. Graves laughed softly. "I'll take any hours you have free and are willing to give me. The children will all be pleased to have the fresh food."

"I'll see you in the morning. Bright and early!"

Thomas cleared his throat again. "I go to work at eight."

"Then I guess I'll be here at eight-fifteen. But that's not very early. I usually start working right after sunup."

Mrs. Graves held her hand out to Joy. "Any hours you can give me. Thank you again."

As Joy and Thomas walked back to the house, Thomas looked at Joy. "You seem to want to do just the opposite of what I say. Did your mother not teach you that it's a woman's place to obey her husband?"

"She told me that yes. And then she winked at me and told me that if my husband told me to do things that made sense, then I should be obedient."

Thomas shook his head. "Oh, dear. I'm going to have my hands full with you, aren't I?"

She clutched his arm tighter and rested her head on his shoulder for a moment. "You are. But it's going to be wonderful anyway."

*****

Right after breakfast the following morning, Joy hurried to the orphanage. She wore one of her older dresses that was more suitable for working in the garden than her new fancy ones, and as soon as she arrived at the orphanage, she pulled off her shoes and socks and left them beside the back door.

Four older boys had been sent out to work with her, and she taught them all exactly what she wanted them to do, explaining how to tell the difference between the tomato plants and the weeds that were woven through them.

All day she spent in the garden on her hands and knees, and when it was time for lunch, she refused to eat the food at the orphanage, realizing she should have brought her own lunch. She couldn't take food from the children's mouths.

By the end of the day, at least some of the garden looked well-taken care of. Though the rest was a bit of a mess. And with the drought they were having, she had the boys switch to watering the garden an hour before she needed to go home so she and Thomas could go to supper with his colleague.

The boys complained that the watering would just make more weeds grow, and she smiled. "Then we get to start all over again! Won't that be nice?"

Joy did her best to watch the time, but it got away from her, and when she realized she needed to be home in ten minutes, she grabbed her shoes and stockings and ran as quickly as she could.

As she ran, she said a silent prayer that Thomas wouldn't be home when she arrived. Her feet and legs were covered in mud, and her old dress would definitely not meet with his approval. Oh, dear. She hoped she hadn't ruined her marriage in less than forty-eight hours, but she knew if anyone could do it, it was her.

*****

Meanwhile, Thomas returned to an unusually quiet house. He loosened his cravat, the day's dealings at the bank having left him with a yearning for solitude and simplicity. He went looking for his wife, though, knowing they needed to leave soon if they were to be on time for supper at Mr. and Mrs. Brookshire's home.

Looking around, Joy was nowhere to be found, and he looked at the clock on the wall, slightly concerned she wasn't yet home from the orphanage.

He'd just decided to go upstairs and change into an evening suit himself, when he heard the door open and saw Joy tiptoeing into the house, carrying her shoes and stockings in one hand, completely covered in mud in a dress that was mere rags.

"Ahem," Thomas cleared his throat, announcing his presence.

Joy stopped where she was. "Sorry. I lost track of time. I'll be ready in a few minutes."

He watched her for a moment. "I'll phone the Brookshires and let them know we were unavoidably detained and will be there within the hour. In the meantime, get upstairs and get out of those rags. Hurry and bathe."

Joy nodded. "I'm sorry!" And she hurried up the stairs.

To say he was disappointed would be putting it mildly, but she was a country girl. And she hadn't hidden her love of dirt and gardening. She was being her true self, and he wasn't sure that he could fault her for that.

An hour later, they arrived at the Brookshires' home, and they were immediately seated. Thankfully, it was only the two couples, and they hadn't kept others waiting.

The maid took them into a parlor there on the first floor, and Thomas introduced Joy. "This is my wife, Joy, and Joy, this is Mr. and Mrs. Brookshire."

"I do hope everything is all right," Mrs. Brookshire said. "It's unlike you to be late."

Thomas nodded. "Yes, Joy volunteered at an orphanage for the first time today, and she lost track of time," he said simply. He wasn't about to tell them they could have made it if they hadn't minded his wife showing up with dirt caked up and down her legs. No one needed to know that detail but him and his servants.

Mrs. Brookshires smiled. "You'll have to join a few committees with me. We're always looking for more volunteers. It will keep you busy until the children begin to arrive."

Joy smiled radiantly. "I do look forward to the children."

"You'll find they bring you a great deal of joy."

"I bring joy wherever I go."

They all laughed at her little joke, and Joy felt as if she were forgiven for her tardiness. Forgiven by everyone but Thomas that was.

Chapter Four

Joy ventured into the kitchen, hoping that Margaret Andrews, the cook, wouldn't mind her sticking her nose in.

"Margaret," she began, "I can't quit thinking about your Beef Wellington. You're going to have to teach me to cook it myself!"

Margaret turned to her. "Is that so? I'll always be here to cook it for you. Unless you're planning to get rid of me."

Joy leaned closer. "But seriously, how do you get that crust so golden? And the filling. I could eat it for every meal!"

Margaret snorted, though the corners of her lips twitched upwards. "Child, you know you're not supposed to be in my kitchen, but I'll show you. Just don't tell Mr. Worthington I let you help cook. I'd never hear the end of it."

As Margaret explained how she made her beef wellington, Joy listened with rapt attention. "See, you want to brush the dough with egg wash, but not too liberally—you don't want a soggy bottom," Margaret explained, demonstrating.

"Nobody likes a soggy bottom," Joy agreed solemnly, then burst into giggles along with Margaret. She felt a great deal more at home in the kitchen with Margaret than she did in the parlor. Better yet was outside in the garden. After a week of marriage, Joy had learned that as long as she was on time and dressed for whatever event Thomas had in mind, he didn't mind her being barefoot and in her old clothes too terribly much.

*****

In his office, Thomas awaited Jonathan Pierce's arrival. Thomas hoped his client would see in Joy the same spark that had ignited something in him.

"Thomas!" Jonathan called out as he entered, extending a hand. "Who is this enchanting creature you've promised to introduce me to?"

"Mr. Pierce, meet my wife, Joy," Thomas said, leading Jonathan back to the parlor where Joy waited, her face still flushed from her time in the heat of the kitchen.

"Enchanted, Mrs. Worthington," Jonathan greeted, bowing slightly with a flourish. "Thomas has told me you possess a...unique zest for life."

"Unique, hmm?" Joy mused. "Well, I suppose that's one way to put it. I prefer free-spirited, but I'll take what I can get."

Jonathan chuckled. "Free-spirited, are you? Yes, I can see why Thomas is taken with you. You're a breath of fresh air in this stuffy city."

"Stuffy? Oh, Mr. Pierce, you haven't seen stuffy until you've tried wearing a corset," Joy quipped, earning a hearty laugh from both men. Of course, she knew better than talking about undergarments in front of men, but she simply couldn't curb her tongue at times.

"I shall take your word for it," Jonathan replied, still chuckling. "And may I say, I am very happy Thomas found you. Anyone who can bring lightness to his life is a treasure indeed."

"Treasure, you say? Well, I did uncover the secret behind Margaret's beef Wellington today. Does that count?" Joy winked at Thomas, who despite himself, couldn't help but smile.

"Most certainly," Jonathan agreed. "Perhaps one day, you'll grace us with a taste of this legendary dish."

"Consider it done," Joy declared. "At our next gathering, it will be Wellingtons all around!" Thankfully, she knew Margaret would be in the kitchen to help.

"Then I look forward to it with great relish," Jonathan said. "And, Thomas, You're right. She's delightful."

As Thomas watched Jonathan head for the door, he knew that he had truly chosen a good wife. She may not be as familiar with society as he'd like, but she was enthusiastic enough to cover most foibles.

*****

"Shoes were not made for this," Thomas muttered, eyeing the uneven dirt path. He looked out of place in his surroundings.

Joy's laughter trilled through the air, clear and bright as the brook they ambled beside. "Nonsense," she chided gently, plucking a leaf from a low-hanging branch and twirling it between her fingers. "Your shoes are merely being introduced to their natural habitat."

"City streets are their natural habitat," he retorted, but there was a twinkle in his eye that softened the complaint.

"Look, Thomas," she said, pointing toward a cluster of wildflowers with her free hand. "The lady's slipper orchids—they're so beautiful!"

He peered at the blooms, their rich pink petals curving gracefully. "I suppose there is a certain charm to them," he conceded.

"Nature is the grandest of teachers," Joy mused, pausing to let a butterfly settle on her extended finger. "It asks for nothing yet offers everything. Tranquility, sustenance, beauty.

"Speaking of sustenance," Joy continued, leading him toward a clearing that opened up to reveal a rolling meadow bathed in sunlight. "I've prepared a surprise." She unfurled a checkered blanket onto the ground and began unpacking a wicker basket.

"Good heavens," Thomas exclaimed, watching as she laid out an array of food.

"Consider this a feast for the soul," Joy announced, patting the blanket beside her. "And for the stomach, naturally."

Thomas settled down beside her. As he took a bite of a sandwich, he realized how different this was from the stilted luncheons he was accustomed to.

"Delicious," he admitted, reaching for a plump strawberry next. Its sweetness burst upon his tongue, unadorned and perfect. "Is this going to be a weekly thing? Or just this once?"

Joy watched, a soft chuckle escaping her as Thomas's eyes widened with each new taste. "Weekly," she said with a grin. "I think there's a certain charm to eating with your hands—I prefer it."

"I suppose," Thomas replied. Juice dribbled down his chin, and he laughed—a clear, unburdened sound that mingled with the breeze. He wiped his face with the back of his hand, looking boyish. "Who would have thought?" Thomas mused. "The simplicity of a picnic could be as good as a restaurant meal."

"I like simpler things," Joy said, her eyes mirroring the blue above them.

"Joy, you're an astonishing woman," Thomas confessed. "You turn what I know on its head, yet somehow, it all makes sense."

She reached over to snag a pastry, breaking it in half to share. "Life is too short for always making sense," she teased. "Sometimes standing on your head is what it takes to make the world interesting."

"Interesting," he echoed, savoring the flaky sweetness of the pastry mixed with her infectious laughter. "That's one word for it."

"Only one?" Joy feigned a gasp. "Thomas Worthington, I shall have to work harder to expand your vocabulary."

"Please do," he grinned. "I suspect you'll be most educational."

As they lay side by side, Joy was at peace. His garden was as big as her father's wheat field, and it was just like being at home.

Later at an opulent restaurant, Joy looked at the perfectly laid out place settings and the white linen tablecloths and napkins.

"Thomas, I don't even know which fork to use first," she whispered.

"Start from the outside and work your way in," Thomas advised with an encouraging smile. "And remember, if all else fails, follow my lead."

The first course arrived, looking more like art than food. Joy hesitated, then sampled a tentative bite, her expression morphing from uncertainty to surprise. "That's...actually quite delicious!"

"Just try everything," Thomas suggested.

"Is this what you eat every day?" Joy asked, her eyes wide as more dishes were presented, each more intricate than the last. She could never eat such fancy foods for every meal.

"Only when trying to impress," Thomas replied. "Although, I must confess, your picnic spread was every bit as impressive in its own right."

"Flattery will get you another sandwich, Mr. Worthington," Joy teased, her confidence growing. With Thomas's gentle guidance, she found herself savoring flavors she never knew existed.

"Joy, you make everything fun," Thomas said. "To new experiences and the company that makes them unforgettable."

"I'll do my best to bring all the *joy* I can to your life," Joy said.

In that moment, surrounded by the sophisticated elegance of Boston's elite, Thomas realized that true joy—his Joy—could turn any situation into an adventure.

After dinner, Thomas gave Joy two pieces of paper. "What are these?" she asked.

"We're going to the theater this evening," he said. "I thought it would be a nice change from all the work you do with the orphans."

The theater was a marvel of velvet and gold. As they settled into their plush seats, Joy glanced around, wide-eyed.

"Is it always this...grand?" she whispered, leaning close to Thomas so only he could hear.

"Only on nights when I bring someone special," he replied.

The curtain rose, and the stage came alive in a whirlwind of drama and comedy. Joy found herself swept up in the story, her laughter ringing clear and bright one moment, her hand clutching at Thomas's sleeve the next, as tears threatened to spill.

"Did you see that?" she gasped during intermission, animated by the spectacle. "The way he professed his love—it was both ridiculous and beautiful!"

"Ridiculous but beautiful seems an apt description for many of life's best moments," Thomas said grinning at her.

*****

Days later, Joy entered the grand ballroom on Thomas's arm. The chandeliers cast a warm glow over the sea of high society, each member more finely dressed than the last. Joy shook with nervousness.

"Remember, just be yourself," Thomas whispered.

"Easy for you to say, Mr. Bank President," she teased back.

But as they mingled, Joy's natural charm shone through.

"Have you heard the one about the farmer's daughter and the traveling salesman?" Joy began, and soon, peals of laughter erupted from the group gathered around her.

Through the crowd, Thomas watched, his heart swelling with pride. Joy had bridged the gap between worlds, turning skeptics into admirers.

"Seems you've stolen the spotlight," Thomas commented later.

"Only because I had an excellent guide," Joy replied, her hand finding his. "I didn't expect making friends in Boston to be quite so...exhilarating."

"Nor did I anticipate enjoying their company so thoroughly," Thomas admitted. "You've turned my world upside down, Joy, in the best possible way."

"And there's no one I'd rather be topsy-turvy with than you, Mr. Worthington," Joy said, her laughter echoing throughout the ballroom.

*****

Thomas led Joy into the heart of the bustling marketplace. Stalls upon stalls stretched before them.

"Good heavens," Joy said, her eyes wide with wonder. The stalls were all multicolored and seemed to blend into one another, creating confusion.

"Quite the artist's palette," Thomas agreed, chuckling at her. His gaze followed her every move as she flitted from one vendor to another.

"Look at these!" Joy exclaimed, pointing to a heap of plump strawberries. She inhaled deeply, closing her eyes.

"Freshly picked this morning," the vendor boasted. "Sweet as the summer sun itself."

"May we?" Joy asked, glancing at Thomas for permission.

"By all means," he said, nodding. The vendor handed them each a strawberry, and together they bit into the ripe fruit, its sweetness bursting on their tongues.

"Divine," she sighed, her voice a song that mingled with the chatter around them.

"Absolutely," Thomas replied.

They wandered past stalls draped in fabrics of silk and linen, their fingers brushing against the cool, soft textures. Joy paused to admire a bouquet of wildflowers, their vibrant hues dancing in the light breeze.

"Wouldn't these look splendid on our dining room table?" she mused aloud.

"Only if you promise not to outshine them," Thomas quipped, earning a playful swat on the arm.

"Flatterer," Joy teased, but she accepted the flowers with a smile.

*****

As they returned home after another joggling ride in the automobile, Joy carried her flowers into the house and put them in a vase before standing back to admire how they looked. "If only I could bring all of the outdoors inside! Our house would be the most beautiful home in all of New England!"

He chuckled, shaking his head. "You bring joy with you wherever you go. Your parents named you well!"

She laughed. "They didn't say that when I was a child. Believe me."

"You weren't always happy as a child?"

She shook her head, taking his hand and pulling him to the parlor with her where they could sit and talk. Her feet hurt from all the hours she'd worn shoes, and she couldn't wait to take them off.

"In my town, they called my brothers and sisters and me the 'demon horde' because we were always playing tricks on people. Or doing other things no one approved of."

His eyes widened. "Like what?"

"Oh, the usual. Snakes in the teacher's desk. Tying a rope to the back of the outhouse, and when she goes inside, pulling the building over. Frogs were a favorite. I remember one time we caught one hundred frogs. I know because it was my job to keep count of them all. And we set them loose in the schoolhouse just before it was time for school to start. My sister lured Miss Allen out the front of the school with a question and we went in the back. When the teacher rang the school bell, it was absolute pandemonium. The girls screamed. The teacher screamed. I think I even screamed for good measure!"

Thomas's eyes widened, but he laughed softly. "Why did you do things like that?"

She shrugged. "I'm not sure. I was one of the youngest, remember? My family already had a reputation by the time I came along, and I just helped perpetuate it."

He shook his head. "Remind me not to let you teach our children about playing pranks."

She laughed. "If they're anything like my family, they'll be born playing tricks on people. We used to throw rotten apples at people who drove by our farm. Sometimes from the apple trees. We were not well-liked."

"I should think not!" he said, shaking his head. "Oh, I worry about our future children now!"

"Oh, you can wait until I'm expecting to start worrying about them. I don't mind."

He chuckled as she leaned down and took her shoes off, wiggling her toes. "Are you going to make my children wear shoes at least?"

"To church!" she said, winking at him. "I can just see them all in little banker's suits and no shoes. Won't they be adorable?"

He sighed. "I have a feeling we're not going to agree about child rearing."

Chapter Five

Joy smoothed down the front of her dress and took a deep breath before stepping into the parlor where her guests were mingling. They were doing a sale of donated artwork for the orphanage, and all of the city's elite were there. She spent most days working for a charity, and many of her nights were filled with trying to raise money for different charities. It was certainly different than her life in Beckham, where she'd spent all her time in the fields.

"Ah, Mrs. Worthington!" a voice called from across the room. "You look positively...quaint this evening."

"Quaint" was not quite the compliment she had hoped for, but Joy beamed regardless, turning to face Jennifer Collins. The other woman wore a gown that shimmered with every step she took, and her nose always seemed to be tilted upward.

"Thank you, Mrs. Collins," Joy replied. "I do believe 'quaint' suits me just fine."

"Indeed," Jennifer said. "But tell me, darling, have you managed to master the art of the waltz since our last gathering? Or will you be sending all the other dancers running for the hills again?"

Joy's jaw dropped a bit in shock that someone would be so outrightly rude to her, and she noticed then that many others were listening intently as they waited for her response.

"Mrs. Collins, you are too much," chuckled a gentleman nearby.

"Simply observant, Mr. Harcourt," Jennifer replied. "We all have our charms, but some, it seems, are more suited for runs through the parks than ballrooms."

Joy felt her cheeks flush. She excused herself, weaving through the throng of guests, toward the quiet sanctuary of the balcony.

"Suitable for runs through the park indeed," she muttered under her breath. "I wonder how she'd react if I challenged her to a foot race." The mere thought of the older woman doing anything that even resembled running made her feel a bit better. She would certainly look a great deal more awkward than Joy did when she was trying to dance.

Her thoughts drifted to Thomas, who would no doubt chuckle at the absurdity of it all and whisk her away for a midnight stroll.

"Suitable for running," she repeated, allowing herself a small, triumphant smile. "Perhaps I'll have them all over for a scavenger hunt and a picnic in the back garden. I'm certain none of them have done anything so physical."

Thomas Worthington did everything he could to stay calm as he approached Jennifer Collins. Thomas's focus was sharp, his intent clear.

"Jennifer," Thomas began. "Might I have a word?"

Jennifer turned, her expression one of practiced ease, a delicate eyebrow arching in curiosity. "Of course, Thomas. What is it?"

"It's about my wife, Joy," Thomas replied. "It has come to my attention that some of your comments were less than favorable." He did his best to control his anger. This woman had no right to insult his Joy.

"Thomas," Jennifer sighed, "I'm simply concerned for our social circle."

"Concern is one thing," Thomas retorted. "But disparaging my wife's character? That's quite another."

"Disparaging?" Jennifer feigned shock, her fan fluttering like a startled bird. "Never! I merely commented on her...unique approach to dancing. If it can be called dancing that is."

"Unique," Thomas echoed. "Joy has many qualities that are more important than dancing. She brings life, laughter, and charm to every room she enters."

"Charm, you say?" Jennifer asked, raising an eyebrow.

"Yes," Thomas said. "She may not know which spoon is which, but she knows how to bring happiness into the lives of everyone she meets. And that is worth more than all the silverware in Boston."

A short while later, tucked away in the quiet corner of the Worthingtons' library, Joy poured out her heart to Thomas in hushed tones.

"Thomas," she whispered. "I overheard what Jennifer said. Am I really such a misfit? I've been trying so hard to fit in."

"Joy," Thomas said. "You are like a breath of fresh air in a stuffy drawing room. To me, you are perfect just the way you are."

"Perfect?" Joy chuckled. "I can't even manage a proper waltz without tripping over my feet."

"Then we shall simply avoid waltzes," Thomas said. "We'll invent our own dance. We'll bring square dances to the Boston elite! Much safer, I assure you."

"Is that so?" Joy's lips curled into a smile. The idea was absurd. "And what would high society say to that?"

"Let them say what they will!" Thomas proclaimed, pulling Joy into a gentle embrace. "We'll be too busy enjoying our picnics and midnight strolls to hear them."

"Picnics and midnight strolls?" Joy mused. "Why, I don't believe we've gone on a midnight stroll yet."

"Well, I don't have to work tomorrow, so after everyone is gone, we'll go for a midnight stroll. It'll be hard for you to be up at dawn after that though!" he warned with a grin.

"I can do it! You have no faith in me!"

"I have all the faith in the world for you."

She took a step forward into his arms and pressed her lips to his. "Thank you for believing in me, even when I can't seem to believe in myself."

*****

The grand hall of the Boston Charity House teemed with the city's elite, a sea of extravagant gowns and tailored suits. Joy and Thomas navigated through the crowd, Joy's simple silk dress a contrast to the dresses those around her wore.

"Are you sure about this?" Joy whispered.

"Absolutely," Thomas replied. "Anytime they make you feel uncomfortable just think about how they would look running through the grass with mud caked on their feet. You could outrun anyone in this room."

As the evening wore on, Joy found herself enveloped in laughter and genuine conversation.

"Thomas," Joy said later, a twinkle in her eye as they watched couples whirl across the dance floor, "do you think they'd mind if we danced the Massachusetts Stomp instead of the waltz?"

"Only one way to find out." With a mischievous grin, Thomas led her to the center of the floor.

Their steps were much different from the others there. They were joyful skips and playful hops, a dance all their own. The room fell silent for a moment, then erupted into cheers and clapping, others joining in the unconventional frolic.

"Joy," Thomas laughed, "you manage to make everyone happy."

*****

Jennifer Collins watched from the edge of the room, her champagne flute poised idly at her lips as Joy Worthington captivated yet another circle of Boston's elite. There was an undeniable sincerity in Joy's eyes. For some reason, Jennifer felt a modicum of respect for the girl.

"Goodness," Jennifer murmured to herself, "am I actually admiring her?"

As if on cue, Joy burst into her infectious laughter, the sound rippling through the crowd. Jennifer felt the corners of her mouth tug upwards. She forced her face into a frown. She didn't care if everyone else in town was falling under the girl's spell. She wasn't going to admire her in any way.

"Enough of this," she whispered with newfound resolve, setting down her drink. It was time for her to step out of the shadows of doubt and into the light of humility.

"Mrs. Worthington?" Jennifer approached.

Joy turned, her smile not leaving her face. "Mrs. Collins! How lovely to see you. Did you enjoy the caviar? I've heard it's positively divine." Not that she would try a bite of the nasty stuff herself.

"Actually, I wanted to speak with you," Jennifer said. She took a deep breath. "I owe you an apology, Joy. I fear I've misjudged you quite terribly."

"Apology?" Joy tilted her head slightly, a lock of brunette curls tumbling over her shoulder. "Whatever for?"

"Your lack of social graces," Jennifer admitted. "But I see now that it's not a lack at all—it's a breath of fresh air in this stifling parlor of pretensions."

Joy blinked, then her face creased into a warm smile. "Well, thank you, Mrs. Collins. That's very generous of you to say."

"Please, call me Jennifer," she offered, extending a hand not just in greeting but in friendship. "And may I support you in any way possible?"

"Of course, Jennifer." The handshake was firm. "And I must say, your candor is rather refreshing too."

"Perhaps we're more alike than different, hm?" Jennifer ventured.

"Maybe so," Joy agreed, her eyes full with humor. "Now, tell me, have you ever danced the Massachusetts Stomp?"

Jennifer chuckled, the sound surprising even herself. "I can't say that I have."

"Then you simply must join us," Joy exclaimed. "It's all the rage in my garden!"

"Lead the way," Jennifer replied. Together, they joined the throng of dancers, their steps unpracticed but their hearts lighter than they'd been all evening.

*****

As Thomas drove the automobile home that evening, Joy was still surprised by Mrs. Collins's about-face. "What do you think came over her to be kind to me instead of simply carrying on as she had been?"

Thomas shrugged. "Perhaps she could see that others genuinely like you. She's never been one to be opposing the group as a whole."

"Maybe..." Joy wasn't so certain. "I'm glad the evening is over though. I think we should go for a midnight stroll in the garden."

He laughed. "Every time we go to a big event now, you think we need a midnight stroll."

She smiled. "I need to be in nature after I've spent so much time with strangers who think they're better than everyone else."

He frowned. "You think my friends all think they're better than everyone else?"

She sighed. "I shouldn't have said it that way...but...it does feel that they look down on me at times. As if I'm a fish out of water, and I must make everyone laugh to pay for my admission. Oh, that isn't fair. I'm sorry I said anything."

Thomas stared straight ahead for a moment after parking his automobile. "Do you really feel that way?"

"Sometimes," she said softly. "I will see people that I know through you as I'm on my way to the orphanage, with my old clothes on, and my hair pulled out of the way with a scarf. I'll greet them, but the women...well, they move their skirts out of the way as if they're afraid that my touch will contaminate them in some way. It's like I'm acceptable if you're with me, but on my own...well, I'm no better than the orphans I work with." She shook her head. "I said that wrong. I don't believe I'm better than the orphans, but I don't believe the orphans or I am less than your friends either."

"But you believe my friends see you as less?" he asked.

"I do."

He frowned. "My world is very different than the one you grew up in, but I don't see it as any worse or any better."

"But you were raised in the life you live in. You've always lived in a fancy house and dressed immaculately. I was raised on a farm, and the clothes I wear to work at the orphanage that we now call my 'rags' were my regular clothes just a few months ago. Will our children be considered less than your friends because they are mine as well as yours?"

"You're imagining things. No one really treats you as lower than them. I've never seen that happen."

"Whether you've seen it or not, it does happen. But it's all right as long as I can spend some time outside after a night with them. I replenish my soul by standing in the garden."

He laughed softly. "You replenish your soul, do you?"

She nudged him with her shoulder, silently chiding him for making fun of her.

"Let's go stroll in the garden then." Thomas was still thinking about what she'd said about his friends looking down on her. He didn't seem to be losing any clients over her, so he shouldn't worry too much, but it was definitely something to think about.

Once in the house, she went straight to the parlor and removed her shoes and stockings. "I'm ready."

He shook his head. "What about your dress? It's going to get dirty."

She shook her head. "I know how to walk like a lady," she said. She stood and walked down the hall toward the back door, one hand holding her dress up off the ground, showing her shapely calves.

"Don't walk like that around other men," he said, watching her. "No one gets to see your legs but me."

She laughed. "At home, I sometimes wore my brothers' old britches, so I didn't have to worry about getting my skirts dirty."

"You didn't!" He knew some women were taking to wearing pants these days, but it had never occurred to him that she was one of them.

"I did. And I'm not even ashamed of it!" She turned abruptly, stood on tiptoe, and kissed him. "My ma wasn't impressed, I'm afraid, but I did it anyway. Skirts get in the way when you're harvesting."

"You, my dear, are just too wild for me. I may have to find myself a nice, simple lady to settle down with."

She shook her head. "Try it. I'll fight her for you!"

His laughter rang throughout the house. "Is that so?"

"It is! I'm not giving you up, Thomas. We belong together."

"Do you think so?" he asked.

She nodded emphatically. "You like to laugh. I like to make you laugh. You like to wear pants. I like to wear pants. See? We belong together."

He put his arm around her as they walked toward the door again. "I think I'm going to need to build you a gazebo in the middle of our garden. That way you have somewhere to be when it rains, and you're too stubborn to come inside."

She giggled. "I have been known to stay out in the rain..."

He sighed. "I should have sent you a questionnaire before I agreed to marry you. Question number one...are you smart enough to come in out of the rain?"

"On occasion," she said, sinking her toes into the grass and closing her eyes as the feeling of being one with nature washed through her.

He watched her soak in the feeling. He was always surprised at how she truly did rejuvenate in the fresh air. He'd heard that some women felt that way when they were around or near water, but never just being outdoors. Of course, he'd not married just "some woman." He'd married Joy, and she had brought him her namesake.

As he stood there, watching her putting down roots in the same way a plant did, he couldn't help but wonder if their children would be like her. Would they have little girls who were rough and tumble and liked to play in the dirt? Or would they have prissy little princesses who couldn't stand a spot of mud?

Either way, he knew he'd be happy. He couldn't really think of sons, because he wanted them all to look just like his Joy.

Chapter Six

Joy stepped through the wrought-iron gate of the foundling home, her hands eagerly slipping into a pair of well-worn gloves. The apple trees were ready to give up their fruit, and Joy was excited to help them do it.

She had seven helpers ranging in size from waist-high to taller than she was. "All right, children," Joy announced with a grin, "today we're going to pick every apple we can find. I'll be up in a tree and so will William, Steven, and Peter. The rest of you pick what you can from the lowest branches." She winked at a freckle-faced boy who was already reaching for the lowest-hanging fruit.

"Miss Joy, look!" squealed a pigtailed girl, triumphantly holding up a bright red apple larger than her tiny hands. "It's as big as a baby's head!"

"Yes, it is, Sarah." Joy laughed. "But let's see if we can find one even bigger, shall we?"

The sun climbed higher as the baskets filled, the children's laughter mixing with the rustling leaves. They worked in a rhythm that made the chore feel more like a dance, passing apples hand to hand, twirling around trees, and occasionally engaging in an impromptu juggling contest that more often ended with giggles than caught apples.

"Miss Joy," huffed a small boy, his basket brimming, "do you reckon we could make the apples fly into the baskets if we had wings?"

"Perhaps," Joy mused, tossing another apple into the basket with a soft thud. "But I think we'd miss out on all the fun of climbing and picking. Wouldn't you agree?"

"Guess so," he shrugged.

*****

The following day found Joy back at the orphanage. She had her shoes off, her sleeves rolled up, and her apron was splattered with what seemed to be more applesauce than what was in the pot. The kitchen was alive with the sweet aroma of cooking apples and cinnamon.

"Miss Joy, it smells like heaven in here!" a little girl exclaimed, her eyes wide as saucers.

"Oh, I don't know. If it's heaven, then that would mean we're angels, and I have a feeling Mrs. Graves would argue with that," Joy said, stirring the large pot of applesauce with a wooden spoon that could have doubled as an oar. "Who wants to help me jar these up?"

Tiny hands shot into the air, and Joy couldn't help but chuckle at their eagerness. The process of canning was meticulous, but the children approached it with gusto, carefully ladling the warm sauce into jars, their tongues poking out in concentration.

"Make sure those lids are on tight," Joy instructed. "We wouldn't want the applesauce goblins to sneak a taste before winter."

"Are there really goblins, Miss Joy?" asked a round-eyed boy, securing his lid with extra vigor.

"Only if you don't eat your vegetables," she replied, earning a chorus of playful groans.

As the last jar was sealed, Joy stood back and admired their handiwork, rows of gleaming jars ready for the shelves in the cellar. She shared sticky hugs with her little helpers, their faces glowing with pride.

"Thanks to you all, we'll be tasting summer long after the snow falls," Joy said.

*****

The following day, Joy returned to the orphanage with a basket of threads and needles. The chatter of children filled the air as she entered the common room, now transformed into an impromptu tailor's workshop. She and Mrs. Graves needed to teach the children how to mend their own clothes, so they could get them ready for school to start in a few days.

"Miss Joy, does this look straight?" asked Tammy, holding up her not-quite-evenly hemmed shirt with a hopeful grin.

"Almost as straight as a ruler," Joy teased before helping to adjust the stitches. Laughter bubbled amongst the children, their small fingers diligently working to keep pace with her.

"Miss Joy, you sew faster than a squirrel gathers nuts!" proclaimed little Annie, her eyes alight with admiration.

"It comes from lots of practice. I never had a new dress until I came to Boston. I always had to take in the seams on my sisters' old dresses so they'd fit me," Joy explained, threading her needle with another swift motion.

When she got home that afternoon, Thomas was waiting for her, and he didn't look happy.

"Joy, my dear," Thomas began, "we need to talk."

"All right. What's wrong?"

"You've spent every day this week at the orphanage," Thomas said, crossing his arms. "And while I admire your dedication, I must remind you that we have responsibilities of our own."

"But these children are also my responsibility," Joy responded, meeting his gaze. "Besides, who else will help them mend their clothes for school? It's hard enough to be an orphan. They don't need to also wear clothing that looks like it belongs in a pile of rags."

"Joy, you're not their mother," Thomas sighed. "You've got a husband who misses spending time with his wife."

"And you've got a wife who finds joy in helping those in need," she retorted. "Surely there's a compromise to be had."

"Perhaps," Thomas conceded. "But what of the dinner parties, the social calls, the clients who expect—"

"Thomas," Joy cut in, "I work hard to make sure I'm home for all the things you need me for. Surely you understand that the children will be starting school in a few days, and things need to be done immediately to get them ready."

"I love your generous heart, but Boston society has its expectations," Thomas countered.

"Then let Boston society learn a thing or two about unexpected joys," Joy declared. "What do you say, Mr. Worthington? Shall we shake up the world together?"

"Shake up the world?" Thomas mused, finally allowing a full smile to grace his lips as he looked into her bright eyes. "With you by my side, Joy, I believe we just might."

The following day, Joy knelt in the orphanage's expansive garden, her hands gently cradling the heavy squash blossoms as she hummed a cheerful tune. Her heart swelled with a blend of pride and affection for the flourishing plants.

She tried to stand, but a wave of nausea seized her. She paused, pressing a hand to her mouth, and Mrs. Graves was by her side in an instant.

"Are you all right?" the older woman asked.

"I shouldn't tell you because Thomas doesn't know yet, but I'm expecting. I plan to tell him this evening." Joy stood up slowly and carefully. "I find the nausea isn't limited to the mornings, though I've always heard it referred to as morning sickness. What a misnomer!"

Mrs. Graves smiled. "I have some ginger cookies in the kitchen. Ginger does wonders for nausea."

"I don't want to take food from the children." Joy shook her head. "I think I may need to stop here for the day, though. Do you think you can guide the children in finishing the harvest of the squash? I'll be back tomorrow to help you can."

Mrs. Graves nodded. "Yes, of course. Go home. But don't forget your shoes this time!"

Joy laughed. "I hate shoes. If Thomas wasn't so insistent that I wear them, you would never see me in them in the summer."

"You're just like the children. I swear little Andrew has lost his shoes fifteen times this summer. I find them all over the garden."

"I knew I liked Andrew," Joy said, smiling. She pulled her shoes on and tied them quickly. "I'll be back tomorrow."

"I don't know what we ever did without you, Joy."

By the time she was home, Joy was feeling sick again. She went into the parlor, removed her shoes, and put her feet up. Her feet were covered in dirt again, but she couldn't do anything about it with how she was feeling.

Thomas found her there an hour later when he returned home. "Are you unwell?" he asked, obviously surprised to find her inside.

"Actually," Joy began, her eyes dancing with secrets, "I believe I'm expecting something that will keep me unwell for a few more months."

"Expecting?" Thomas echoed. "You mean—"

"A child, Thomas." Joy's face glowed with happiness. "Our own little sprout!"

Thomas gaped at her for a moment, obviously thrilled. "A child!" he exclaimed. "Oh, this is wonderful news! But you must rest, no more gallivanting off to orphanages or tending gardens. You'll stay home where it's safe."

"Safe and sound like a winter apple, eh?" Joy teased, though her heart sank at the thought of being confined. "But the children—"

"Were fine before you started helping there, and will be fine when you stop," Thomas insisted.

"Thomas, I'm not some weak woman who can't work," she protested. "I will lose my mind if I stay inside, and you know it."

Thomas knew arguing with Joy was pointless. With an affectionate shake of his head, he relented. "Just promise me you'll be careful?"

"I wouldn't do anything to risk our child," she said. She stood up and put her arms around his neck. "We're going to have a baby!"

He laughed, wrapping her up in his arms. "I couldn't be happier."

*****

The next day, true to her word, Joy supervised the children at the orphanage as they gathered tomatoes. A small army of eager hands plucked the ripe fruit, each child competing to see who could pick the most.

"Careful with the squashes, Johnny, they bruise easier than your knees," Joy said.

"Like this, Mrs. Worthington?" Mary held up a perfectly selected squash for inspection.

"Perfect," Joy praised. It was hard for her to watch the children work without helping, but even Mrs. Graves expected her to sit on a blanket and watch the harvest without helping.

After the harvest, Joy returned to the orphanage kitchen, sleeves rolled up and apron donned, ready to tackle the mountain of produce.

"Watch the fingers, Samuel. We're making tomato sauce, not finger stew," Joy quipped.

With each jar sealed and labeled, Joy felt a sense of accomplishment. As much as she knew Thomas wanted her at home, she felt so much love being there at the orphanage. It was hard to leave the children.

When she got home a few hours later, she was excited about all they'd accomplished, explaining what they'd done that day to Thomas. "Perhaps our little one will inherit my love for gardening!"

"Or for bending rules," Thomas responded, arms folded and an amused smile playing on his lips.

"Only the ones that need a bit of...flexibility," Joy replied.

*****

Thomas paced the length of the parlor, hands clasped behind his back and brow creased in a tight frown. The grandfather clock in the corner ticked away with maddening precision, each second a sharp reminder of Joy's absence. He'd all but begged her to stay home more, especially now with their child on the way, but it seemed his words evaporated like morning mist against her resolve.

"Joy," he began as soon as Joy breezed through the door, her cheeks flushed with a telltale rosy hue from her day's exertions. "We need to talk about your...activities."

"Thomas, you worry too much!" Joy laughed. "The children needed me at the orphanage."

"I need you too," Thomas interjected. "My clients require attention too, attention I cannot give when I'm fretting over whether my wife will grace us with her presence or not."

"Ah, but I am here now, am I not?" Joy countered with a playful smile.

Before he could formulate a response, the doorbell rang, its chime echoing through the house like an indictment. Thomas glanced at the clock, his shoulders sagging—a full half-hour early. He waved for Joy to hurry upstairs to get ready as he walked toward the door and his clients.

"Mr. Applebottom, Mrs. Applebottom, welcome," Thomas said, extending his hand as he led the couple into the parlor. "Please forgive us. My wife is still preparing. I assure you she will be down soon."

"Preparing?" Mr. Applebottom's brows rose in thinly veiled surprise, his gaze lingering on the staircase as if expecting Joy to appear in a flourish of skirts and apologies.

"An unexpected delay at the orphanage where she volunteers," Thomas explained. "You know how these charitable endeavors can be."

"Indeed," Mrs. Applebottom replied, her tone as crisp as the lace at her throat. "One must always prioritize, Mr. Worthington. Especially in times such as these."

"Absolutely," Thomas agreed.

The minutes stretched, filled with idle chatter about business and the weather, all the while Thomas listened for the sound of Joy's footsteps. Finally, he heard her footsteps on the stairs.

"Mr. and Mrs. Applebottom," Joy greeted, her voice infused with warmth as she extended her hand. "I do apologize for the delay. The day ran away from me, as they often do when there's work to be done."

"Work?" Mrs. Applebottom repeated, the word hanging between them.

"Yes, I do enjoy being busy," Joy said, turning her smile to Thomas. "My husband has told you of the children at the orphanage? I find it so rewarding to spend my days there with them."

"Children do have a way of capturing one's heart," Mr. Applebottom admitted,.

"They do," Thomas found himself saying. "And my wife has a particular gift for helping there."

As the conversation turned to tales of Joy's adventures at the orphanage, Thomas watched, a reluctant smile tugging at his lips. Perhaps there was room in their lives for both business and benevolence, after all.

They all moved into the dining room, and Joy took her seat at the foot, smoothing her skirts under her.

"Isn't that right, Joy?" Thomas said.

"Absolutely," Joy affirmed. She had no idea what Thomas was talking about as she'd been thinking about the other couple's horrible last name and not paying attention.

Mrs. Applebottom sniffed slightly and adjusted the string of pearls at her throat. "I must say, Mrs. Worthington, your punctuality could use some...refinement," she said.

"I do apologize once more," Joy replied, her voice sugared with a sincerity that she hoped would defuse Mrs. Applebottom's displeasure. "The garden was particularly generous this year, and the harvest waits for no one."

"A garden, you say?" Mr. Applebottom asked, obviously interested.

"Oh, yes!" Joy beamed. "I've been helping with the harvest and canning of the fruits and vegetables grown in the orphanage's garden.

And their apple orchard. I'm afraid it's taken up most of my time this week."

"It's good to instill the value of an honest day's work in children," Mrs. Applebottom remarked.

"Teaching them is a communal effort," Thomas added quickly.

"Quite commendable," Mr. Applebottom nodded.

Joy exchanged a look with Thomas. As dinner progressed, Joy's infectious enthusiasm seemed to gradually thaw the frosty exterior of Mrs. Applebottom, who, despite herself, began to inquire about the varieties of apples grown in the orchard.

"Who knew apples could be such common ground?" Joy thought.

The cook deftly navigated the dining room, balancing a serving platter piled high with roasted chicken as the aroma of herbs wafted through the air.

"I must warn you, this chicken has been known to cause people to fight over the last pieces," Joy said.

"Is that so?" Mrs. Applebottom inquired, eyeing the chicken curiously.

"Indeed," Joy replied. "Thomas can hardly keep himself from sneaking into the kitchen whenever Margaret cooks this recipe."

"Margaret does have a magic touch with chicken," Thomas chimed in.

"Ah, then we are in for a treat!" Mr. Applebottom exclaimed.

As they ate, Joy regaled them with lighthearted tales of her escapades at the orphanage, each story punctuated by her laughter and the delighted chuckles of her guests. "And there I was, apron full of squirming kittens, trying to convince the children that the kitchen is not the place for them."

"Good heavens!" Mrs. Applebottom gasped, her lips twitching in amusement as she envisioned the scene. "And what became of the kittens?"

"Adopted, every last one," Joy beamed. "Though I dare say, they left their little paw prints all over our hearts—and the pantry!"

"Charming!" Mr. Applebottom declared, dabbing his mouth with a napkin as he leaned back in his chair.

"How wonderful," agreed Mrs. Applebottom.

As dessert was served—a decadent apple tart, naturally—Joy told of her latest gardening adventure, involving an ill-timed encounter with a child holding a watering can.

"Water everywhere, and not a drop on the tomatoes!" she said with a laugh. She neglected to mention that her legs were covered in mud by the end because she knew Thomas wouldn't approve. "It was a big mess, but no one minded too much because the child with the watering can was doing her very best. And the tomatoes were picked just this morning, and they did beautifully."

By the end of the evening, the Applebottoms were completely charmed with Joy and her tales of helping at the orphanage.

"Mrs. Worthington," Mrs. Applebottom said, "you have turned what I anticipated to be a rather ordinary evening into something quite exceptional."

"Joy has a special way of doing that," Thomas added fondly.

"Yes, she does," Mr. Applebottom agreed, raising his glass in a toast. "To unexpected joys and delightful company."

After they were gone, Thomas looked over at Joy. "I don't know how you did that. They were so angry when you weren't ready when they arrived, but they loved you by the end of the evening."

"Stories about children make everyone happy," Joy said, smiling.

Thomas wasn't so certain, but he simply hugged her to him. She really did bring everyone joy.

Chapter Seven

The harvest was finally over at the orphanage, so Joy headed home, pleased with herself that they'd been able to put up so much food for the winter for the orphans. She felt as if she'd just climbed the tallest mountain or fought a grizzly bear with no help.

She got home just as Thomas was arriving after his day at the bank. "We're finally finished!" she said, her voice full of celebration.

"Does this mean I'll get my wife back?"

"Bet you never thought you'd see the day," Joy teased.

Thomas turned to Joy, "Why don't we celebrate the season's close with a visit to the sea? We could be within an hour's drive from your parents' place."

Joy's eyes widened. "Oh, I would love that so much! It feels like it's been a decade since I saw my parents!"

"Let's do it then," Thomas replied. "I look forward to meeting the parents of my sweet bride who is more comfortable covered with mud than clean."

Joy quickly wrapped her arms around Thomas and kissed him. "I can't wait!"

"I've already arranged some time off from work. We'll leave Friday."

"Would you mind if I telephoned my sister, Elizabeth, so she can let them know that we're coming?"

"Of course not." Thomas had never dreamed she wouldn't just pick it up and use it without permission. What was she waiting for?

"I'll call her tomorrow then. Oh, I can't wait to hear her voice. Though, I've never spoken on the telephone. Will her voice sound the same?"

Thomas nodded. "Yes, it will mostly sound the same. Do you need me to teach you to use it?"

Joy shook her head. "No thank you. I'm certain I can figure it out."

*****

They decided they would go visit her parents on their way to his family's house on the ocean. On the day of the visit, Joy emerged wearing a pretty silk dress that flowed around her like a gentle stream. Its delicate fabric caught the sunlight, casting shimmering patterns onto the wooden floorboards of their home. Thomas watched her descend the stairs, a tender smile gracing his lips.

"Look at you," he remarked. "Your parents won't recognize you."

Joy blushed faintly. "I just want them to be proud that I'm not running around barefoot covered in mud any longer."

"So, you're going to deceive them?" he asked, grinning.

As for Thomas, he had rummaged through his wardrobe for something less...Bostonian. He settled on a pair of well-worn jeans and a button-up shirt which felt odd. Topping off the ensemble was a cowboy hat, which he adjusted awkwardly atop his head, its brim casting a shadow over his earnest face.

"Will this do?" he asked, turning to Joy uncertainly.

She bit back a laugh, thinking he looked sweet, but out of place. "You look fine, Thomas. But you don't have to dress differently for my parents."

"I don't want to seem unapproachable to them," he said.

"You'll fit right in wearing that," she assured him with a bright smile. "Come on, cowboy. I can't wait for you to meet my parents."

*****

As they got out of the buggy they'd rented in Beckham, Joy thought about how different the two of them looked. Normally, she'd be the one in the country clothing, and he'd be the one looking like he just stepped out of a ballroom.

"Look at us," she chuckled. "I'm all dressed up like I'm going to a ball, and you're dressed for a rodeo."

"Seems we've swapped roles for the day," Thomas replied with a crooked grin. "But, if we're mismatched, my dear, we're mismatched together."

"My parents probably won't even notice," Joy said, looping her arm through his as they made their way to the modest farmhouse.

The sight of the homestead struck Thomas more profoundly than he'd anticipated. The wooden slats of the house were worn and sun-bleached, windows patched here and there with paper where glass should have been. He'd realized she hadn't grown up with wealth as he had, but he hadn't realized her family was quite as poor as they obviously were.

"Your childhood home?" he asked.

"Yep, every creaky floorboard and leaky roof tile," Joy said. "It's not much, but it's filled with love and laughter."

Thomas suddenly felt as if the Worthington mansion, with its grand halls and beautiful decor, was sterile in comparison to this living, breathing home.

"Love and laughter..." he mused aloud. "Perhaps that's the true wealth." Joy carried with her a happiness he'd never seen in another person. Perhaps money wasn't the way to feeling fulfilled and happy.

"Come on," she urged with a smile, tugging him toward the front door. "My mama is probably looking out the window at us, wondering if we're going to stand here like a couple of statues all day."

As they approached, the screen door swung open, and a chorus of voices welcomed them. Joy squealed as she saw her younger sister, Ida Mae, and hugged her close. "I feel like I haven't seen you in years!"

Ida Mae stared at Joy for a moment. "You don't look much like my sister, but you sure sound like her. You should change into something more comfortable while you're here. No point in ruining that dress."

Joy laughed, and the sound seemed to fill the entire house. "Unless I'm out milking the cows or slopping the pigs, I think this will be just fine."

Ida Mae sighed. "I think you should change. I can't look at you that way and think of you as my sister."

Thomas watched in quiet amazement as Joy deftly slipped away, only to reappear moments later dressed in an old, sun-faded dress that clung to her like a second skin. The transformation was startling.

"Ready for the real fun?" she chirped, her hands on her hips as she flashed him a mischievous grin.

"Define 'fun,'" he replied.

"Come along," she beckoned, leading Thomas to the barn where the cows awaited. She settled onto a stool beside a large spotted cow and began milking. Each squirt of milk into the pail seemed to pull her further from him.

"City hands could never," she teased over her shoulder.

"Is that a challenge, Mrs. Worthington?" Thomas asked, rolling up his sleeves with mock determination. His attempt at milking was less than successful—eliciting laughs from Joy and a disdainful moo from the cow.

She demonstrated the right way to do it for him, and slowly, he grasped the concept and finished milking Bessie, who was the daughter of a cow that had once been painted purple by Joy's older siblings.

"You did it!" Joy said, excited that he'd even been willing to try. He was out of his element, but he seemed to be taking it all in stride.

A litter of kittens tumbled across the barn floor, their tiny mews filling the air with innocence. Joy sat on the ground, allowing the furry babies to climb over her, their claws catching in the fabric of her dress as she giggled.

"You're truly happy," Thomas murmured. "You're like a different person here."

"Maybe this is the real me," she said, a kitten perched precariously on her shoulder.

It was hard for him to reconcile the girl who had managed to get much of Boston society eating out of her hand with the woman who was enjoying sitting on the floor of a barn covered in kittens.

They made their way back to the house, just in time for supper. The kitchen was warm and fragrant, a stark contrast to the orderly, impersonal culinary operations back at the Worthington estate. Joy's mother stood at the stove, stirring a pot of something that seemed to be little more than broth and vegetables.

"Smells delightful, Mrs. Miller," Thomas offered, his stomach rumbling.

"Nothing fancy, just some garden stew," her mother replied, placing a steaming bowl before him with a nurturing smile. "Eat up. It'll warm your bones."

"Who knew carrots could taste so sweet," he remarked, chasing another bite with a piece of crusty bread.

"Everything's sweeter when it's grown with love," Joy answered. "That's our secret ingredient."

"Then consider me thoroughly charmed by the Miller family recipe," Thomas said.

As they ate, Joy watched him with her family, realizing he fit in better than she'd imagined he would. She couldn't help but feel proud of her banker from Boston.

"Mama, one of the reasons we came is to tell you we're expecting."

Mrs. Miller smiled at her daughter. "I figured you would be soon. No one in the family seems to be able to marry for more than a few months without getting in the family way."

After supper, Thomas slumped back against the worn leather of the buggy seat, a bemused smile playing on his lips as Joy guided the horse with ease.

"Never thought I'd find myself feeling this..." Thomas struggled for the right word. "Content, just sitting here listening to the crickets."

Joy chuckled, her eyes still on the path ahead. "It's so much more tranquil here."

He nodded, considering her words.

"Today was good for you, wasn't it?" Joy asked. She was back in her silk gown and she seemed so out of place with the leads of the buggy in her hands.

"Surprisingly, yes," Thomas admitted. "I never imagined I'd take such delight in watching chickens or...what was that game you played with the kittens? 'Pounce and tumble'?"

"Something like that," she said, her laughter coming easily. "It's not exactly a game with rules more than it is giving them a bit of exercise."

"It looked like fun." He paused, then added with mock gravity, "I fully expect our future offspring to be champions at it."

"Only if we're raising them on a farm," she teased.

"Speaking of raising," Thomas ventured. "Your family...they were so welcoming, so full of life. I thoroughly enjoyed my day with them, despite how different it is from what I'm used to."

"Did you?" She glanced at him with a smile.

"There's something about the simplicity of their lives that's very...appealing," he said.

"Appealing enough to trade in your suits for overalls?" Joy asked.

"Let's not be hasty," he replied with feigned alarm. "A man can appreciate the way another man lives without wanting to join them."

"Of course," she agreed. "But it wouldn't hurt you to get some dirt under your nails once in a while."

"Perhaps," Thomas conceded. "Though I must say, I've never slept better than I do after a day of fresh air and honest work. You've shown me that."

"See? You're practically a farmer already," Joy said.

"Let's not go planting crops just yet," he replied, chuckling softly as he reached for her hand, giving it a gentle squeeze. "But today? Yes, it was perfect."

Joy smiled. "I thought so too."

"Your folks seem to always be calm," Thomas observed. "I couldn't help but notice they didn't exactly leap for joy at the news of us expecting."

Joy chuckled. "Thomas," she said with an affectionate shake of her head, "when you're the fourteenth child born to parents, and your older siblings have turned childbearing into a competitive sport, the announcement of yet another grandbaby isn't exactly unexpected."

"Fourteenth." He rolled the number around his tongue like a foreign concept. "It's hard for me to even think of having that many children."

"It didn't bother me," Joy said. "At last count, Mama said there were thirty-two grandchildren. Or was it thirty-three? Even I can't keep track of them all."

"Family gatherings must be chaotic," he mused.

"More like a circus," Joy confirmed with a laugh that held a note of pride. "Of course, the family is spread across the country now. There are only six or seven of us still in Beckham. Elizabeth has sent out lots of our siblings as mail-order husbands and wives."

"I think I'll feel very out of place."

"You're not allowed," she teased. "The best thing you can do is bring your appetite and a sense of humor. Miller gatherings are not for the faint of heart."

"An appetite and a sense of humor," he repeated. "I believe I can manage that."

"See?" Joy nudged him playfully. "You're adapting already. By the time our little one arrives, you'll be ready to join the ranks of the Millers."

"I'm not sure of how true that is," he said. "But I'll certainly do my best to fit in." He raised his hand and pointed off into the distance. "There it is. It's not much, but my family has always vacationed there."

Not much? Joy shook her head. "I don't know how you can take that kind of wealth for granted."

He shrugged. "You get used to it eventually."

Chapter Eight

Joy's eyelids fluttered open, and for a moment, she simply lay still, savoring the warmth of Thomas's arm draped over her. She'd never been at the ocean before, and it surprised her just how calming the sound of the waves were as they lapped against the beach.

After a moment, Joy wriggled from beneath the comforting weight of his arm, slipping out of bed. She tiptoed toward the door. She wanted to make him breakfast in bed, feeling the need to treat the man who worked so hard.

"Where do you think you're sneaking off to?" Thomas's voice stopped her short. She halted mid-step.

Joy turned, smiling as she saw him looking up at her. He looked so sweet wearing just the sheet. "I thought I'd get a start on breakfast," she said.

Thomas propped himself up on one elbow, the corners of his mouth lifting into an amused smirk. "You're planning to cook?" he asked, one eyebrow arching in playful skepticism. He was constantly surprised by the whirlwind of energy that was his wife. Even morning sickness didn't seem to slow her down...much.

"Yes, I am," Joy declared with mock indignation. "And I'll have you know, Mr. Worthington, that my culinary skills are quite—"

"Remarkable?" he finished for her.

"Exactly," Joy agreed. "So you just stay put, and prepare to be impressed."

Thomas chuckled. "Well then, Mrs. Worthington, dazzle away. But know that I am fully capable of assisting my talented wife, should she require it."

"Assistance noted," she replied with a cheeky grin. "But first, I have a feast to create."

Joy's fingers had barely grazed the doorknob when Thomas's voice stopped her in her tracks.

"Before you transform our humble abode into a culinary paradise," he began, sitting up against the headboard, the sheet down around his waist, "there's something you ought to know."

Pausing, Joy turned. "Oh?"

Thomas's lips curled into a knowing smile. "We have Mrs. Dunfrey. She comes in every morning I'm here. Cooks, cleans, and generally ensures that I don't fall to pieces."

A wave of surprise washed over Joy, followed swiftly by a twinge of disappointment. "A housekeeper?" she murmured.

"Yes." He nodded sagely. "An excellent one at that. But that just means we'll have more time together."

But Joy could not help but feel useless. Her shoulders drooped, and she gave Thomas a rueful smile. "I suppose it's lovely to have fewer chores," she conceded, "though I can't shake the feeling that I should be doing...something constructive. I guess I should have brought the mending from the orphanage. I hate to be idle."

"Dearest Joy," Thomas said warmly. "Your company alone is worth more than you realize. We can simply enjoy ourselves. Is that so difficult?'"

"I suppose not. But I really do enjoy being busy. I haven't learned how to spend my time reading novels or sitting around doing nothing. I'll have to find a worthwhile endeavor to stay busy here at the beach. I wonder if there's an orphanage nearby. It's too bad it's so late in the season, or I could find someone who needed some gardening help."

"Think of it as an opportunity," Thomas suggested. "An opportunity to explore new pursuits, perhaps?"

"New pursuits," Joy repeated thoughtfully. "Yes, that might just be what I need."

"Whatever you choose," Thomas said with a gentle chuckle, "I have no doubt it will be nothing short of remarkable."

"Flatterer," Joy said, shaking her head.

"Merely a husband speaking the truth," he replied with a grin.

Joy explored the storage room Thomas had pointed out to her the night before, her mind set on her newfound mission. The scent of salt and old wood welcomed her as she rummaged through a tangle of fishing gear. With a triumphant grin, she unearthed two rods and reels that seemed promising.

"Ah, here we are," she murmured to herself, giving one of the reels a test spin. It whirred satisfactorily, and she felt a surge of excitement at the prospect of sharing this slice of ordinary life with Thomas, who had likely never baited a hook in his life.

"Joy?" Thomas's voice floated from the doorway. "What are you plotting now?"

"Plotting? You make me sound like a child who is always involved in some sort of nefarious scheme, and I can assure you, I'm not." She turned, feigning innocence while holding the rods. "Merely planning an educational excursion."

"Into the wilds of the beach, I presume?" he teased.

"Exactly!" Joy beamed. "You, my dear husband, are going to learn the noble art of fishing."

"Am I now?" He raised an eyebrow but stepped forward. "And what will be my first lesson?"

"Patience." She winked and moved past him. "But before that, we need bait."

Thomas watched, bemused, as Joy walked outside with purpose, the hem of her old dress swishing determinedly. In the soft earth near the water's edge, she began to dig for worms, her fingers deft and unbothered by the dirt clinging to her skin.

"Should I have brought a book, to study this 'patience' you speak of?" Thomas called out.

"Nope." Joy glanced over her shoulder. "You'll learn by doing. And speaking of doing—" she held up a wriggling worm triumphantly "—your first catch of the day!"

"Charming," he said.

"You know, you could come and help me dig for worms. I'm just a woman after all, and I am expecting your spawn."

"Spawn? You make me feel as if any child I have will be evil."

Back inside, Joy frowned. Her skirts wouldn't do for such an endeavor—a snagged hem or a dunk in the sea would ruin the dress.

"Thomas, where do you keep your oldest trousers?" she called out.

"Second drawer," came the shouted reply.

She found an ancient pair of his pants, the fabric softened by countless washes. Holding them up, she marveled at how huge they would be on her. But she quickly changed out of her dress and into the oversized trousers, cinching them tight with a belt pulled to its last notch.

"Ready?" she asked, emerging from the room with a flourish.

Thomas choked back a laugh, covering it with a cough. "Are those mine? You look...adorable."

"You think? I promise these are necessary for our activity and not a fashion statement." Joy patted her hips, the pants huge on her. "Now come along, Mr. Worthington. The fish await."

He offered his arm, which she took with mock solemnity, and together they headed toward the shore.

Joy cast her line with practiced ease, reaching up to push her hair from her face. She'd tied it back, but the wind was strong and kept blowing it around. Thomas stood beside her, his brow furrowed in concentration as he mirrored her movements.

"When you feel a pull, you've got a bite," she instructed. "I've already informed the housekeeper that we only eat what we catch for supper. So, if we catch nothing, I'm afraid we shall go hungry."

"Seems easy enough," Thomas replied. "And I'm not letting you go without supper while you carry my child."

"Then you'd better catch something, because I refuse to eat anything but fish tonight."

"If all else fails, I'll get the net from the storeroom and catch fish with that!"

She shook her head. "It's sort of like a game of cat and mouse. You have to stand still and not move until you feel that bite on your line."

"Or a banker awaiting the perfect investment," he countered with a grin.

"Exactly!" she said. They stood in companionable silence for a while.

"Joy, I believe something is pulling on my—" Thomas began, his voice trailing off as he was interrupted by a sudden tug on his line. His eyes widened. "Is this—?"

"Reel it in!" Joy urged, excitement tinting her words.

With a mix of panic and exhilaration, Thomas cranked the reel handle, reeling in his catch with clumsy enthusiasm. His actions resembled more of a wild dance than any sort of fishing technique.

"Steady, Thomas! Steady!" she called out, trying not to laugh at him.

Finally, with a triumphant whoop from Thomas, a decent-sized cod flopped onto the shore. Thomas looked at the fish, then at Joy, a boyish glee lighting up his eyes.

"I caught a fish!"

"You did," Joy praised. "And a fine one at that. But now we need more."

They spent the day casting lines and sharing laughter, Joy explaining the nuances of fishing, and Thomas learning as much as he could. It was obvious to her that he was enjoying the new endeavor. Even as he fumbled with slimy worms and slippery fish, his laughter mingled freely with hers, a sound as bright and clear as the sea itself.

Shortly before suppertime, they gathered their fishing gear and their catch for the day to take it all inside. Joy watched as Thomas held up their string of fish.

"Shall we take these to the kitchen?" he asked. He seemed excited to show off their handiwork.

"Absolutely," she agreed.

Mrs. Dunfrey raised an eyebrow at the sight before her. "Well, well," she commented dryly, "the master of the house has turned fisherman, has he?"

"Only with the best of teachers," Thomas replied.

Mrs. Dunfrey set to work, cleaning and preparing the fish with skilled hands. The aroma of cooking filled the kitchen, mingling with the satisfaction that comes from a meal hard-earned.

When they sat down to eat, Thomas took his first bite, a look of genuine surprise crossing his face. "I never knew fish could taste this good," he admitted.

"Everything tastes better when you catch it yourself," Joy said.

"Perhaps," Thomas mused, "but I suspect it has more to do with the company."

*****

Joy and Thomas sat side by side in the sand, enjoying the rhythmic crash of the waves. Joy's toes wiggled freely, a contented sigh escaped her as she rested her head on his shoulder. "You did a good job fishing today. Soon, I'll have you gardening and hunting with me, and you'll forget how to work on ledgers."

"Seems to me you're trying to turn me into the kind of man you would have married if you'd stayed in Beckham."

Joy laughed at that. "No man in Beckham would have had me. That's part of the problem of being part of the demon horde. No one particularly believes you can outgrow your misdeeds. That's why my family is scattered far and wide. We couldn't seem to outgrow our reputations."

Thomas shook his head. "I have a hard time believing that no one would have married a woman as beautiful as you are. It makes no sense."

"Well, would you want to marry a woman who you knew might lock you in an outhouse for no other reason than it amused her?"

He frowned. "You wouldn't do that."

"No, but I did as a child. And that's what people know of me. And don't think you're the only man who has ever seen me running around in britches that I had no business wearing. Half of Beckham thought I would never be able to settle down and have a family. There's only one of us left unmarried, and that's Ida Mae. I wouldn't be surprised if she had to go all the way to Seattle to find a husband."

"Seattle?" he asked.

She nodded. "Elizabeth didn't start her business. No, she took it over from a woman who went to Seattle as a mail-order bride herself. So, when I think of far away, I rarely think of other countries. I think of how far away Seattle is."

As if on cue, the first drop of rain plopped onto the sand between them, the dark spot quickly multiplying as more drops joined. Joy turned her face upward, a giggle bursting out. She stood, holding out her hand to Thomas. "Come on, let's enjoy this!" She wanted to dance with him in the rain, but she had a feeling he would protest.

Thomas took her hand, allowing himself to be pulled to his feet. They strolled back toward the house, laughter mingling with the sound of the downpour. Raindrops were drenching them, but they didn't rush. Instead, they savored the moment, the freedom, and the sheer joy of the day they had shared.

"Who would have thought a day of fishing could lead to such revelry?" Thomas quipped, shaking his head as water droplets flew from his hair.

"Life is full of surprises," Joy replied, grinning up at him. Her dress was soaked through, clinging to her legs as they walked, but she didn't care a bit. "Especially when you're willing to get a little wet."

Upon reaching the house, they found refuge under the covered back porch, settling their drenched bodies onto the porch swing. They sat and watched as the storm transformed the ocean into a wild tempest. Joy felt as if she was one with nature, the pulse of the storm moving through her body.

"There's something about the rain," she said after a moment. "It washes away all of yesterday's mistakes, leaving a clean slate so I can make all new mistakes tomorrow. And we all know there will be more mistakes every single day."

"Your optimism is infectious," he said, chuckling lightly. "I think I'm starting to see the world through your eyes, and I must say, I like it."

"Ah, but don't let it fool you," she said. "I plan on teaching you to garden next. In fact, you should build me a greenhouse in our back garden so I can start soon. Imagine how much I could grow if I had the whole year to do it."

"You think I have the skills to build a greenhouse?" he asked, raising an eyebrow.

"Oh, no. Of course not. You'd probably maim yourself if you tried to hold a hammer. No, I mean you should pay someone to build me a greenhouse. That way it would be done properly."

He sighed. "I know you're right. But I did like it when I thought you thought I could do it!"

She laughed softly. "You get the greenhouse built, and I'll make sure you know how to garden in it. Isn't that a great compromise?"

"I suppose so. Though, I worry I don't have the green thumb you do."

"That's all right. At least it won't be black and blue as it would be if you tried to build it yourself."

He nudged her with his shoulder. "You could be nicer to me."

"I could. But where's the fun in that?" she asked, winking at him.

"Maybe for tonight, we should just watch the rain."

As she sat beside him, feeling positively electrified by the storm around them, she knew she was right where she wanted to be.

Chapter Nine

"Home sweet home," Thomas declared as they came into view of the house after walking home from the train station.

"Why does it always feel so good to be home?" Joy asked. "I'm going to miss how relaxed we both were at the beach, though."

"You weren't relaxed! We spent half of our time finding something constructive for you to do!"

"And the other half was spent lounging around as if we had no care in the world!"

"But I've made arrangements to ensure you'll have a piece of nature with you, even here in Boston."

"Arrangements?" Joy's brow arched in curiosity. She knew the man was up to something, but she had no idea what. Perhaps he'd arranged for them to move outside the city, which would make her the happiest woman alive, but she would miss their beautiful garden and all the children at the orphanage. She wasn't sure she wanted to move to the country after all.

"Yes," Thomas said. He led her through the wrought-iron gate toward their garden—or what once was their garden. Now it was a bustle of activity as men worked to erect a building made of glass.

"Thomas, is that...?" Joy began, her hands coming up to cover the gasp that escaped her lips.

"A greenhouse," Thomas confirmed, grinning at her. "Now you can dig in your glorious dirt year-round."

"Goodness, you are full of surprises," Joy said with a laugh, her mind already thinking of what she wanted to grow first.

"Only the best for you," Thomas said. He wouldn't tell her, but he was almost as excited as Joy was. The idea of having fresh foods on his table year-round was something he looked forward to.

"Shall I fetch my gloves and join them?" Joy teased.

"Perhaps let them lay the foundation first," Thomas chuckled, wrapping his arm around her shoulders. "There will be plenty of time for digging in the dirt."

"Plenty of time..." Joy repeated dreamily, watching as the skeleton of the greenhouse took shape before her very eyes. "Oh, Thomas. This is the absolute best present you ever could have given me. I can't wait to get in there and dig in the dirt. What should I grow first?"

"Whatever you choose to grow, I will happily eat. Unless it's flowers. I'm afraid I'm not terribly fond of eating flowers..." Thomas said, guiding her back toward the house. "It's going to be another couple of weeks before it's done, so you'll have plenty of time to decide what to grow first."

"Of course," Joy agreed, though her gaze lingered on the greenhouse. "We just need them to work quickly. I know I have a lot to do already, but that dirt is calling my name. Quite loudly actually. I'm surprised you can't hear it!"

With a laugh, Thomas led her into the house and up to their room. "I'll let you get the first bath after being on that train."

"Do you find trains dirty, Thomas?"

"Terribly."

"Then let's just share the tub. I'm quite sure it's big enough."

Thomas didn't have to be asked twice. He left a trail of clothing to the bathroom.

*****

Joy stood at the window watching as the final pane of glass was hoisted into place on the greenhouse.

A smile played on her lips as she pictured little hands from the orphanage reaching for the fruits of her labor.

"Thomas already thinks I've lost my mind," Joy mumbled to herself with a chuckle. "He'd better not catch me staring at the greenhouse with an excited look on my face. He'll think he's been replaced!" With a last look at the nearly completed greenhouse, she turned away.

The basket sat by the door, a woven sentinel stuffed with garments in need of mending from the orphanage. Swiping it up, Joy settled herself in the parlor, threading a needle with practiced ease. She may not have enjoyed working indoors, but she was quite good at it, and she was determined to use every skill she had to help the children from the orphanage.

As she stitched, the house was quiet, save for the occasional creak of wood and distant hammering from outside. Joy's thoughts wandered back to the greenhouse and the joy it would bring her to dig in the dirt and to harvest food she could share with the orphans. No longer was she the person who received charity. She was able to help others, and soon, she could help them even more.

She sighed. "I'm sitting here daydreaming of carrots. It seems I am one step away from becoming a vegetable myself," she quipped to the empty room.

"Who are you talking to?" Thomas's voice drifted in from the hallway.

"You now," Joy replied, not missing a beat as she tied off a knot and snipped the thread. Joy laughed, holding up the mended shirt. "This could be worn by two or three more boys."

"I suppose it could. Too bad you don't take such care of me," Thomas said with a playful sigh.

"You have plenty of servants to take care of you. What do you need with a wife?"

"Then I suppose I'll have to brush up on my charm," he replied, walking over to plant a kiss atop her head. "I'm sure you won't even remember I'm here once you have that greenhouse."

"Your assistance is most welcome," Joy said, her tone grandiose, "I'm sure to remember you if you help me with the planting. Of course, you'll have to be careful not to trample all my hard work with your...extraordinarily large feet!"

"Trample? I'll have you know I have the utmost grace," he protested.

"Of course," Joy agreed with a grin, "as graceful as a bull in a china shop."

"Very well, I accept your challenge," he declared. "I shall become the most delicate gardener Boston has ever seen."

"Then it is settled," Joy concluded. "I shall be the head gardener, and you shall be my lackey."

"I don't think I agreed to lackeyhood..."

"It was implied..."

*****

Joy sat at her customary place by the parlor window, trying to finish up all the mending that the orphanage needed done before her greenhouse was ready for planting. A stack of neatly repaired garments lay beside her, each destined for the children who had unknowingly carved a place in her heart.

"Joy," Thomas's voice carried a hint of amusement as he entered the room, "I fear you might be giving Mother Goose a run for her money with all this sewing."

She glanced up from her work. "Oh, Thomas, I'm simply doing my part. Instead of spending my afternoons away, I've brought the mending here." Joy patted the pile of clothes. "A compromise, if you will, so that I may be near you and still lend a hand to those in need."

"Ah, a compromise," he said, shaking his head. "And here I thought you were starting a garment factory right under our roof."

"Would that be so terrible?" she teased, threading her needle.

"Only if it involves throngs of people in my home," he said, crossing the room to rest his hand on her shoulder. "But I must admit, your industriousness is quite charming."

"Charming enough to overlook the bits of thread scattered about the house?" Joy asked.

"Consider them a colorful addition to the decor," Thomas replied.

As the laughter between them subsided, Joy set aside her sewing and stood, feeling the weight of her belly reminding her of the life flourishing within. Her gowns had grown snug around her midsection, and she knew it was time to adjust her wardrobe to accommodate her changing figure.

"Speaking of charm," she began, patting her belly, "it appears I'll be needing to make some alterations of my own."

"Your dresses are becoming rather tight on you."

"Are you calling me fat?" she asked, turning to face him and narrowing her eyes.

He held his hands up in self-defense. "Never! But our child is becoming rather plump. Wouldn't you agree?"

She eyed him, trying to decide if she should be offended or not. "She does seem to be growing quickly," Joy agreed. "It seems our little one wishes to announce her presence to the world."

"Then we shall ensure *he* does it in style," Thomas declared. "You'll have the finest maternity wardrobe Boston has ever seen."

"I don't need new clothes," she said. "I just need to let out the seams of those I have."

"Joy, we can afford a maternity wardrobe, and it would cut down on your workload a great deal," he told her, wrapping an arm around her shoulders.

She shook her head. "I'd rather spend the money on other things. There's no need for me to buy something new. You know I'm always looking for more work to do."

*****

Joy's hands fluttered over the bolts of fabric in the store. The aisles of the Boston marketplace were awash with pre-Christmas vibrancy, bustling with patrons.

"Excuse me," Joy said, sidestepping a gentleman. "Could you point me toward the toys?"

"Right past the lace, dear lady," the shopkeeper called from behind the counter.

"Thank you!" she called back, weaving through the crowd.

Once she was in the aisle with the wooden soldiers and porcelain dolls, Joy let out a soft sigh of delight. Her fingers moved over a miniature tea set before settling on a stuffed bear with a comically oversized bow around its neck. "You'll be perfect for little Susie," she murmured, tucking the bear under her arm and picking up a toy sailboat. "And this, for Samuel."

"Planning to start a toy shop?" Thomas's voice carried over the hubbub.

"Only if it means I can play with the stock daily," Joy replied without turning, adding a spinning top to her growing collection.

"Ah, but where would we put our toy shop? The greenhouse has taken prime real estate," he teased, coming to stand beside her.

"Speaking of which," Joy pivoted to face him, "it's finished. And it's beautiful, Thomas. It feels like I've been granted my own little patch of Eden."

His smile deepened at her words. "I'm glad to hear it. I might not know much about dirt, but I understand it makes you happy."

"Ecstatic," she corrected, placing a final doll into her basket. "And I'm not the only one who'll benefit. Imagine the joy on the children's faces when they see what we've brought them."

"More joy than watching me attempt to garden?" Thomas quipped.

"Far more," Joy confirmed with a laugh, leading the way to the counter to pay.

*****

Joy was excited to dig in the dirt in her very own greenhouse that weekend, and Thomas had donned an old pair of pants to assist with the planting, although his efforts seemed to result in more soil outside the pots than in.

"Remind me again why we couldn't hire a gardener for this bit?" he grunted.

"Because," Joy said, patting down the earth around a young tomato plant, "there's a certain satisfaction in doing it yourself. Plus, I enjoy your company."

"Even if my company comes with an atrocious gardening technique?"

"Especially then," she assured him. "It's endearing."

"Endearing," Thomas echoed, straightening up with a mock frown. "I'll have that etched on my tombstone: 'Here lies Thomas Worthington. His gardening was atrocious but endearing.'"

She laughed. "For now, let's focus on keeping these plants alive instead of thinking of our future tombstones, shall we?"

"Agreed," he said, offering her a hand to stand. "After all, we've got plenty of growth to oversee—plants, children, and...us."

"Us," she echoed. "But it seems that I'm the only one growing." She looked down at her burgeoning belly with a sigh.

"Should I start trying to grow as well?" he asked, looking down at his own flat stomach.

"Let's not get ahead of ourselves," Joy retorted.

*****

"Starting a side business in children's attire, are we?" Thomas asked, quirking an eyebrow as he picked up a velvety blue scrap of fabric. "I suppose the same people who buy toys will buy the clothes, so we can sell them both in the toy store."

Joy looked up, her cheeks rosy with warmth. "Oh, Thomas! You startled me," she said. "No, it's not a business. These are for the orphans. For Christmas."

"Ah," he nodded, understanding dawning upon him. "I see you've taken to playing Santa Claus."

"Someone must ensure they have a merry Christmas," she replied, her voice tinged with resolve. "Can you imagine? Little faces lighting up at the sight of new clothes?"

"I can. And I reckon they'd light up even brighter with even more toys to accompany those fine frocks and trousers," Thomas mused. A thought struck him then. "What say I contribute to this yuletide cheer?"

Joy's eyes widened. "Would you? That would be wonderful, Thomas!"

"Very well. Operation 'Cheerful Orphanage' is underway," he declared. "I shall procure the necessary...what do boys fancy these days? Rocking horses and... bicycles?"

"Those sound perfect!" Joy exclaimed. "They would love them."

"Then it's settled." He donned his coat with a flourish. "I'll venture into the wilds of Boston toy stores. Wish me luck."

"Good luck, my brave knight," she teased, waving him off with a grin.

The bell above the toy store door jangled merrily as Thomas stepped inside. The place was crammed with wonders—a veritable treasure trove for any child.

"Can I help you, sir?" asked the shopkeeper, emerging from behind a fortress of teddy bears.

"Yes," Thomas replied, adjusting his cufflinks. "I need...let's start with bicycles and rocking horses."

"Right away, sir!" The shopkeeper seemed delighted by the idea of a sizable order, rubbing his hands together.

"And add anything else that might cause a boy's heart to race with excitement," Thomas added.

"Of course, sir. We've got spinning tops, cricket bats, and train sets that would do just the trick!"

"Perfect," Thomas agreed.

"Will there be anything else?" the shopkeeper inquired as he tallied up the order.

"Let's not forget the marbles. No boy should be without a proper set of marbles," he decided on a whim.

"Marbles it is," the man echoed, adding them to the list. "Will that be all?"

"Of course not!" Thomas said. "We must have toys for the girls as well."

"Just tell me what you'd like to spend, sir. We'll have it all delivered before Christmas Eve."

"That will be perfect," Thomas said, naming a figure that had the shopkeeper's jaw dropping. As he exited the shop, he couldn't help but feel that this may very well be the most satisfying investment of his career.

Thomas strolled through the garden, a path he had walked countless times, yet this time with a spring in his step and an idea blossoming in his mind. The greenhouse stood proudly, its glass catching the early morning sun—a beacon of Joy's passion for nurturing life from the earth.

As he approached the back door, he could already hear the clatter and commotion coming from the kitchen. It was music to his ears—the sound of Joy humming along to the rhythm of her baking.

"Thomas, is that you?" Joy called out, her voice rising over the din of pots and pans.

"Of course," he replied, leaning on the doorway and watching her dust flour off her apron. "I see the bakery has come to us."

"Three days of baking," she stated matter-of-factly, a smudge of frosting highlighting her cheek like a badge of her dedication. "These treats won't make themselves! And I couldn't ask dear Margaret to do extra work for Christmas!"

Thomas couldn't disagree with her. "And speaking of making...there's something I wish to discuss with you."

"Does it involve more sugar? Because we're running dangerously low," she said.

"Something far sweeter," Thomas said. "I want you to choose an orphan from the home—someone to bring into our lives permanently. For Christmas."

Joy's hand froze mid-whisk. Then, just as quickly, her face softened into a smile so warm it rivaled the oven's heat.

"Thomas, are you certain?"

"More than I've ever been," he assured her, stepping closer.

"Choosing one, though... How can I possibly—"

"Choose with your heart, my dear Joy. You have more than enough to share," he encouraged.

"Then we'll need another stocking," she mused, already lost in thoughts of which child might soon call their house a home. "It will be hard to choose just one..."

"Stockings, bicycles, marbles...We'll need a bigger mantle," Thomas teased.

"Help me with these trays, will you?" Joy motioned toward the counter.

"Only if I get to sample the goods," Thomas bargained. He thought about how much he'd changed since their wedding in June. In six months, he'd learned to garden—albeit poorly—and now he was helping in the kitchen. He'd never dreamed he would do either of those things before, and now they seemed like they were normal things to do.

"Deal," she said, passing him a cookie. "But only one, or we won't have enough for the children."

"Of course, just one," he agreed, although they both knew his resolve would crumble like the sugar cookie in his hands.

Together, they worked in harmonious disarray, the kitchen a whirlwind of flour, sugar, and laughter. And as each cookie was placed on the tray, they thought of the child who would eat it. Christmas would be glorious!

*****

The first light of Christmas morning barely tinged the Boston skyline as Thomas and Joy, bundled against the cold, stood before the towering wrought-iron gates of the orphanage. They'd brought a horse-drawn wagon full of presents with them, eager to give them to the children.

"Ready to play Santa and Mrs. Claus?" Thomas asked, his tone teasing but his hand squeezing hers with affection.

"Only if you're prepared to be outdone by Mrs. Claus's superior gift-giving abilities," Joy shot back, a playful glint in her eye.

Thomas chuckled, the sound mixing with the jingle of keys as he unlocked the gate. "I must concede, your cookies have probably already made us the heroes of the day."

"Ah, but your bicycles might just turn us into legends," she countered with a grin.

They navigated the cobblestone path leading to the main building, their arms laden with bundles of sweets and toys. The early hour meant the children would still be nestled in their beds, visions of sugar-plums—or Joy's gingerbread men—dancing in their heads.

They walked to and from the wagon many times leaving everything just outside the door.

Joy paused at the door, her heart fluttering like the wings of a hummingbird. "Do you think they'll like the rocking horses?"

"If they don't, I suppose you'll have to take up riding them yourself," Thomas said.

"Ha! A sight that would be. Me, atop a miniature steed, leading a cavalry of orphans into battle against imaginary dragons," Joy said. "And my stomach would undoubtedly be the first to arrive."

"An unbeatable force, no doubt," Thomas agreed.

Their entrance roused the matron from her office, her stern look softening at the sight of the couple's festive intentions. "Mr. and Mrs. Worthington, to what do we owe the honor?"

"Christmas, Mrs. Graves," Joy replied, her voice warm as freshly baked bread. "We've come bearing gifts for the children."

"Gifts and the promise of adopting one lucky soul today," Thomas added.

"Adopting? My word..." The matron was visibly moved, dabbing her eye with the corner of her apron. "That is a gift beyond measure."

"Let's get all the gifts inside," Joy suggested. "We have an entire mountain of presents just outside the door."

Mrs. Graves looked as if she was the one receiving the gifts. "We'll put them in the living room around the Christmas tree!"

The three of them worked quietly to bring all of the toys inside. Finally, the scene was set, and they were ready for the orphans.

"Should we wake them, or let them get up on their own?" Joy asked.

"Oh, we need to get them down here!" Mrs. Graves said. "You two can't waste your entire day here."

"Sure, we can," Joy said. "But I'd rather spend it playing with the children."

"Lead the way," Thomas said.

At the top of the stairs, Joy hesitated, her hand resting on the doorknob to the girls' bedroom. "Do you think they'll be surprised?"

"Joy, my love, between your baking, the clothes, and the toy-laden satchel, these children are about to have their best Christmas ever." Thomas couldn't help but smile at her enthusiasm.

"Then let's make some merry," Joy declared, and with that, she swung open the door.

A chorus of gasps and sleepy murmurs greeted them as they entered the dormitory, the girls rubbing their eyes in disbelief.

"Good morning, little ones!" she exclaimed. "Who's ready for Christmas?"

"Santa!" a small voice squeaked from the back.

"Mrs. Claus, actually," Joy corrected with a wink. "And my dashing assistant, Mr. Claus."

"Assistant?" Thomas feigned indignation, earning a round of laughter from the girls.

"Very well," Joy conceded. "My equal partner in holiday merriment. Now, go wake the boys!"

Chapter Ten

A chorus of excited gasps and giggles filled the air as Thomas brought in the last of the gaily wrapped parcels.

"Go on then," he urged. "Open them up!"

The children pounced on the pile of presents. The room bloomed into a kaleidoscope of torn paper and ribbon, each child revealing a treasure that was theirs alone.

Joy watched the whole thing, laughing as one young boy, no older than six, hoisted a toy soldier high above his head with pride.

"Look, Mr. Worthington! He's just like you, all serious and stuff!" the boy exclaimed.

As the children delved deeper into their newfound wonders, Joy's gaze wandered from face to face. She searched for...something. Someone. She wanted to find the child who needed her the most to share her home and life with. But how could she possibly choose?

"Did you find what you were looking for?" Thomas asked, leaning closer to whisper in her ear, his eyes following her searching gaze.

"Almost," Joy replied. "There's a child here who needs us, Thomas. I can feel it."

"Then we'll find them," he assured her, placing a hand on her shoulder.

"Yes, we will," she said, her eyes finally settling on a figure sitting slightly apart from the rest—someone who wasn't tearing into a present or brandishing a new toy sword. Joy's maternal instinct, strong and unerring, told her that this was the child her heart had been seeking.

"Let's make this a Christmas to remember, shall we?" Joy whispered, a plan forming in her mind.

"Absolutely," Thomas agreed. "After all, isn't that what the season is all about? Making memories and sharing love."

"Sharing love," she echoed, making her way toward the child, ready to gift not just a toy or garment, but a family, a home, and a future filled with possibilities.

Joy approached the girl, whose eyes darted up from the patchwork quilt she'd been absentmindedly running her fingers over. Madelyn—Maddie, as they called her —looked like she was bracing herself for a lecture.

"Madelyn," Joy said, her voice gentle, "how would you feel about spending your next Christmas surrounded by your very own family?"

Maddie's mouth opened slightly, no doubt expecting to hear something else entirely. "My own...family?" she asked, a flicker of hope igniting in her eyes.

"Yes," Joy confirmed with a warm smile. "Thomas and I would be honored if you would consider being a part of ours."

"Really?" The word trembled on Maddie's lips.

"Absolutely," Thomas chimed in. "We've got plenty of room, and we're told our Christmases are pretty special."

Maddie's gaze bounced between Joy and Thomas. Her posture softened, and she allowed herself a tentative smile.

"Then, um, yes," she stammered. "Yes, I'd like that very much."

"Marvelous!" Joy exclaimed, clapping her hands together. "Let's gather your things, then. It's time to take you home!"

*****

The Worthington mansion loomed grandly as the wagon rolled up the cobblestone drive. Maddie stared; her eyes wide with wonder. She'd heard stories about places like this, but never dreamed she'd be calling one home.

"Welcome to your new home," Thomas announced as he helped her down from the carriage.

"Goodness," Maddie muttered to herself, taking in the sprawling gardens and the stately columns. "It's like a castle."

"Wait until you see inside," said Joy, guiding Maddie through the grand entrance. They passed George Langley, the gardener, who offered a gruff nod and a rare smile, recognizing the importance of the moment.

"Your room is just up these stairs," Joy said, leading Maddie to the second floor. The door swung open to reveal a sunlit space, complete with a four-poster bed, a writing desk nestled by the window, and shelves waiting to be filled with books and treasures.

"Mine?" Maddie asked.

"Yours," Joy affirmed. "And no textile mills in sight," she added with a wink, knowing the common fate of orphans Maddie's age.

"Thank you," Maddie whispered. "I won't let you down."

"The only thing we expect you to do is to be yourself," Thomas assured her.

"Exactly," Joy agreed, wrapping an arm around Maddie's shoulders. "Now, why don't we give you some time to settle in? There's much to explore, and dinner will be ready before you know it. Margaret's cooking is something truly special."

"Or to write in your new journal," Thomas added, nodding toward the desk where a leather-bound book awaited its first entry.

Maddie's eyes shimmered with unshed tears, a mixture of joy and overwhelming relief. "I think I'm going to like it here," she said. "Where is the kitchen? I'll go down and help with dinner."

Joy smiled. "They won't even let me help with dinner. I can promise you, they won't allow a child in their precious kitchen."

"But...You're keeping me from the mills. I need to earn my keep."

"You're our daughter now. No need to earn your keep. We'll enroll you in school after the holidays are over," Thomas said.

Very softly, Joy whispered, "Welcome home. I hope you'll love it here as much as we do."

"Then I reckon I've come to the right place," Maddie said.

Maddie stood in the middle of her new room, clutching a rag doll, which she'd brought to the orphanage with her after her parents had died when she was only four. The wallpaper was a soothing shade of sky blue, and the bedspread featured a delicate pattern of wildflowers that reminded her of Joy's smile—warm and welcoming.

Joy smiled. "We'll leave you to settle in. We'll be downstairs in the parlor. If you can't find us, just call out."

"Thank you," Maddie said, her voice a whisper of awe. "I always...I wanted to be a teacher. But I thought..."

"Thought what?" Joy prodded gently.

"That it was impossible," Maddie sobbed. "That I'd never have the chance."

Joy patted her back, a twinkle in her eye. "Well, life's full of surprises. You're in a house where impossible is just another word for 'not done yet.' You can be anything you want to be."

*****

The days following Christmas passed like pages in a storybook, each moment filled with newness and light. Maddie, determined to prove her worth, threw herself into helping with every chore, from dusting the bookshelves to helping in the greenhouse.

Her eagerness was met with raised eyebrows and amused glances among the staff, but no one could deny the joy that seemed to dance in her steps.

"Reminds me of Joy when she first arrived," Thomas mused aloud to Jonathan Pierce, who had stopped by for an impromptu visit.

"Ah, yes, a whirlwind of curiosity and barefoot wonder," Jonathan agreed, leaning back in his chair and sipping his tea. "Madelyn appears to be cut from the same cloth."

"She really is," Thomas said, watching as Jonathan paused to admire a portrait of Joy and himself. "Though I suspect she'll keep her shoes on more often."

"I would hope so," Jonathan laughed. "Easier on the feet."

Joy, meanwhile, found Maddie's company a refreshing change of pace. The girl's laughter was infectious, and her desire to help, albeit occasionally clumsy, was endearing.

"Maybe tomorrow we can pick out some fabrics for new school clothes?" Joy suggested as they sat together in the parlor.

"Really?" Maddie's face lit up like the sun breaking through clouds. "Oh, Mrs. Worthington, I'd like that very much!"

"Call me Joy," she corrected gently. "Or I could take you to my modiste and have the dresses made for you. I think maybe that's what we'll do. I want to spend my days digging in the dirt, not sewing."

"Joy," Maddie repeated. "Thank you, Joy."

*****

At the orphanage, Maddie helped Joy distribute afternoon snacks to the children. She always wanted to help, no matter what was happening around her.

"Mrs. Worthington—er, I mean, Joy," Maddie said with a shy smile, "I can't believe how different every day feels now."

Joy handed her another tray of cookies. "I can only imagine. Having you with us brings us so much joy."

"Before," Maddie hesitated, her voice dropping to a whisper, "I thought for sure I'd have to work in one of the mills. They say it's loud as thunder all day long and the air is so thick with lint you could knit a sweater from what sticks to your clothes."

"Knitting sweaters from mill air doesn't sound like the most comfortable pastime," Joy said.

Maddie's gaze lingered on Joy's rounded belly. "I'll help out. Whatever you need."

"Sweetheart," Joy said, taking Maddie's hand. "You are part of our family now. You have all the rights and love we will give this baby.

Thomas and I want you to have every opportunity to chase your dreams."

"Really?" Maddie asked. "But people only adopt older orphans to work for them."

"Not us," Joy reassured her. "We're hoping to keep you from having to work so hard. You deserve a childhood. You have the right to follow your dreams!"

Maddie's eyes sparkled. "Like teaching," she said.

"Exactly," Joy smiled.

"Joy?" Maddie asked, a playful glint in her eye.

"Yes, dear?"

"Could we maybe bake some cookies tomorrow?" Maddie asked. "I love to bake."

Joy nodded. "I think that's a wonderful idea."

Joy watched Maddie chatter away among the children, her laughter a melody of newfound joy.

*****

Thomas turned at the sound of footsteps, and there she was—Joy, with her customary whirlwind energy, somehow softened today into a gentle breeze.

"Thomas," Joy began, hesitating only for a moment before crossing the room to join him. "We need to talk about us."

"I suppose it was bound to happen at some point." Thomas led her to the sofa and sat down beside her.

"Ever since Maddie came into our lives, I can't help but wonder if we're ready for all of this."

"Ready?" Thomas echoed. "I'll admit, the thought of fatherhood is downright scary at times."

"Exactly," Joy said, moving closer to him. "But it's not just about Maddie, is it? It's about you and me, too."

"True, we were strangers when we married," Thomas conceded. "But, Joy, we enjoy each other's company, and I think we're truly meant to be together."

"I do agree. I think we'll make wonderful parents for both Maddie and this little girl we're expecting."

"Our little *boy* will have all the love he ever wants," Thomas agreed. "I never realized that I could find so much joy in being married to a woman who can't remember to wear shoes for the life of her." He nudged her bare foot, which was peeking out from under her skirt.

Joy laughed. "Do you think we can make this work? Truly?"

"Joy," he said, "we've been making it work for (they'd been married six months before Christmas)months now. You've turned my life upside down, and I wouldn't have it any other way."

"Even with the chaos I bring?"

"Especially with the chaos," Thomas affirmed. "And as for making our marriage work, I am wholly committed to this journey with you."

"Obstacles like Maddie's penchant for mischief and my unorthodox ideas?" Joy asked.

"Those aren't obstacles," Thomas replied, his own eyes twinkling. "They're adventures. And I dare say, I'm looking forward to each one."

"Then I suppose we agree," Joy said. "Have I told you that I love you yet?" She'd known for months, but she'd been unsure if he would be accepting of her feelings.

"I don't believe you have. Have I told you yet that I love you?"

"I know you haven't. Why not?"

"Why haven't you told me?"

"I wasn't sure you'd want my love."

"I can't think of anything I want more." Thomas leaned down to kiss her forehead. Joy moved closer to Thomas.

"Thomas," she said. "I can't help but feel like the luckiest woman in all of Massachusetts."

"Only in Massachusetts?" Thomas teased.

"All right, perhaps all the country," Joy conceded with a playful nudge against his chest.

"There's the spirit!" Thomas chuckled "And what do you suppose makes you so fortunate? Is it my dashing good looks or my impeccable financial acumen?"

"Neither," Joy answered. "It's just you."

"I never imagined the girl who stomped all over my feet in our first waltz would also be the woman who fills me with so much joy."

"My name should have told you that!"

He chuckled. "I have to admit, I've never met a woman who was quite so aptly named."

Epilogue

Joy looked down at the baby nursing at her breast, feeling as if her heart would burst with happiness. Thomas had been right all along, and they'd named their son Anthony.

She looked up as the front door opened and closed to see Maddie rushing into the parlor to join her. The girl who had once seemed so shy to her was coming out of her shell.

"How was school?" Joy asked.

"It was good. But that James Jordan made fun of my hair again. He said that having braids makes me look like I'm seven and not fourteen. How can I get him to be nice to me? Hitting him over the head with my textbooks just isn't working!"

Joy laughed. "Hitting people rarely works. Just keep looking at him with doe eyes and make him think you have feelings for him. If he likes you back, he'll stop his nonsense. If he doesn't, he'll run away."

Maddie giggled. "Or—we could get me those pointy-toed shoes I like so much, and I can kick him with all my strength!"

Joy grinned. "I'm all for it, but I'm not sure your father would approve..."

Thomas stepped into the doorway of the parlor. "What wouldn't I agree with?"

"I think Mama should get me some pointy-toed shoes for kicking James Jordan when he teases me, but Mama doesn't think you'd approve."

Thomas laughed. "How on earth did I once think you were a sweet girl who would never cause me any trouble?"

"Just confused I guess," Maddie said, getting to her feet and pressing a kiss to her father's cheek. "I love you, Papa!" With those words she was gone, running up the stairs to put her schoolbooks in her room as she did every day after school.

Thomas stood watching Joy feed Anthony. "I'll never get tired of watching you with him," he said softly.

"I feel the same. Oh, Thomas, I never dreamed I would be so happy married to you. I need to write Elizabeth and tell her thank you."

"I already did that."

"I have too," she confessed. "But what would it hurt to write her once more?"

He laughed, sitting beside her on the sofa, and wrapping an arm around her. "Our life is perfect."

"It's everything I've ever dreamed it could be!"